WHAT ARE WE DOING IN LATIN AMERICA?

(A Novel about Connecticut)

by Robert Riche

THE PERMANENT PRESS
Sag Harbor, New York

Library of Congress Cataloging-in-Publication Data

Riche, Robert, 1925–
    What are we doing in Latin America? / by Robert Riche.
        p.   cm.
    ISBN 1-877946-01-X : $19.95
    I. Title.
    PS3568.I333W4   1991
    813'.54—dc20   90-43908
                                                           CIP

Manufactured in the United States of America

THE PERMANENT PRESS
        Noyac Road
    Sag Harbor, NY 11963

To Fran

CHAPTER I

I am sitting here on the throne in the downstairs bathroom trying to decide whether it would be more dignified to shuffle ten feet across the tiles to the closet and fish out a roll of toilet paper from the bottom shelf, or call out for help to my wife who I can hear in the upstairs bathroom over my head, standing, it sounds like, in front of the mirror, most likely in her robe and bunny slippers, putting the finishing touches to her lips and eyelids.

It's a big decision, because I am trying to do everything these days the way someone like, say, Donald Trump would. With charm, but at the same time, with firmness of purpose—and, most of all, with dignity. At least, not shouting, for Christ sake. Or arguing. I am very, very conscious of my dignity lately, ever since the president (CEO) of the company I work for, and whom I report to, told me in the hall outside his office two weeks ago that I lack it. Dignity.

"Are you kidding, Frank?" I said. We're on a first name basis, and until that moment I had thought we were on fairly informal and friendly terms. Which, of course, was my mistake, because thinking that, somewhere along the line I obviously must have had the bad judgment to stop worrying for a moment or two about how I looked or was acting in front of him, and must have dropped my guard sufficiently to let slip some kind of smart remark that I probably thought was hilarious at the time that maybe didn't go over all that well. Maybe this happened more than once. As a matter of fact, I can recall at least one instance, now that I think of it, sitting in his office and looking at him across that scallop of desk he presides over, and becoming aware that although his lips were pursed into something resembling a smile, he was managing to frown at the same time, as though experiencing gas.

Anyway, obviously his perception of me was different from my perception of myself, which was quite a shocker, as I have never thought of myself before now as not being dignified. As a matter of fact, my perception is that I tend to make a fairly strong and favorable impression on most people. I have a good height, being a little under six feet, reasonably trim, slightly heavier than I'd like to be, but at my age of 49, a few days away from 50, it gives me a kind of substantiality that I confess I'm rather fond of, suggesting perhaps a gourmet's appreciation of a decent bottle of wine and a nicely prepared veal chop in a light cream sauce. I have a college education, a liberal arts degree from Amherst, which I value as highly as Frank does his business degree from Lackawanna School of Business & Finance. I play a fair game of tennis. I ski. I try to keep up on world affairs. I try to read contemporary fiction, and not just the best sellers. I even work at reading the poems in *The New Yorker.*

Still, the awful part is, he could be right.

Otherwise, how explain the fact that even as I ponder these matters astride the throne my mind is conjuring up a scene in which he is here in my house—which he is not, of course—and walks in on me in the bathroom—because the door is not

6

locked (in fact, it is ajar)—and catches me with my pants
down to my ankles hobbling over to the closet for the toilet
paper (because I have almost decided now not to call my wife)
and I turn and see him there, and instead of cringing and
covering up and making silly gulping ingratiating noises as
any normal human being come upon in such circumstances
would, I simply hoist my hind quarter haunch just a fraction of
an inch higher, and flash the old moon right in his face.

Forty-nine years old, practically 50, an Amherst graduate,
an executive, and I have thoughts like that.

Well, a crap's a crap, and not a bad time to ponder the
darker side of one's consciousness, when you get right down to
it. As I am doing now, and apparently with a somewhat
salutary effect on the old bowel, too, as I take a deep breath,
press, exhale. Uh-h-h-h-h. Oh, boy. Wow. Now, there's dignity for you. And a real pleasure, I don't mind saying. In fact,
what else is there in life, really, as downright satisfying?

Which is an indication in itself—the fact that I pose such a
question—of the low point to which I have sunk. I am depressed. Generally. Or maybe just apprehensive. Thinking
about things—of my son, in particular, the uneasy suspicion
growing that we are not going to have an easy time with him,
now that he is fifteen, going on sixteen.

Fear for his future well-being is with me often these days,
and particularly at this moment, as we prepare to drive him
today up from Fairfield County along the rural back highway
that follows along the banks of the Housatonic River to the
sanctuary of an Eastern prep school that we were able, with
some difficulty, to get him accepted into.

We are leaving in an hour. Which explains perhaps better
than anything else the loose bowel. Also, the crimped feeling

in the middle of the chest, the roiling intestine, the shifty eyes, and racing pulse. It means so much to me, and to my wife, to have it work out.

But, even so, back to the immediate urgent concern. I am faced with making a decision that will get me up off the throne and back into the world of action again.

In the wicker wastebasket under the sink directly in front of me, I descry two, no, three! pieces of crumpled Kleenex, relatively clean except for some lipstick smears on them the color of my daughter's "pink frost lip gloss." By rolling forward on the balls of my feet and extending one arm to perch a fist on the floor in a lineman's crouch I can reach in and pluck the tissues out, shaking loose a couple of strands of entangled blonde hair, and I have just solved my most immediate dilemma, and if not in the most dignified manner, at least, no one will ever know, thereby proving the old New England adage of my mother's, "Where there's a will there's a way." Also, "Necessity is the mother of invention." Probably there are a couple of others.

My son is in his room, at this moment filling the old camp trunk we hauled out of the attic for him. His room is apart from the house, in the space which we had converted into a loft, over the garage. Well, the garage below isn't really a garage anymore, either, since my wife three years ago appropriated it as her photography studio. (As a consequence, my car, and hers, too, both sit in the driveway in front of what is now the downstairs studio/upstairs loft bedroom, bleaching under the glare of summer sun and rusting out in winter's ice, snow and salt.)

Pants buckled up now, I am debating whether it's too early to go out and offer to help my son with his trunk when the question is decided for me by a sudden blast of sound coming from his room, 180 decibels of "The Grateful Dead" descending over our lawn and proclaiming to the neighbors on both sides that it will be a few hours yet before his departure. (I *think* it's "The Grateful Dead," though it could be "Rush.")

I get out to the garage-upstairs loft bedroom fast, because I know that the phone will ring in another second or two, with Chet Dowd, my next-door neighbor, the airline pilot, calling to ask (in a nice way, though with an unpleasant whine in his voice, not at all, I don't imagine, like the mellowed-out tone he must reserve for announcing the weather and altitude over the intercom system of the Boeing 747 that he flies) if there isn't something I can do about tuning down that racket from my son's room.

This has happened before, more than once. I don't blame Chet. If his kid, who is only eight, were to blast the airwaves with his stereo I probably wouldn't like it any better than Chet does. Better that he should call me than call the cops (anonymously), and then have the cops cruise into the driveway in one of their black and white patrol cars with the lights flashing.

("We've had a complaint, sir—" "What's that? You'll have to speak up, officer. I can't hear you!")

Chet is a nice guy. Really. When we moved into our house six years ago, it was Chet who ambled over while we were in the midst of moving a stove up the back steps and ceremoniously draped around my wife's neck a lei of only slightly wilted blossoms, which he explained to both of us is the traditional symbol of greeting in Hawaii—as if we hadn't ever watched television, or before that, Pathe newsreels as far back as 1950. The lei was made of real flowers, and he claimed he had been keeping it in the refrigerator just for us since his

9

return from his last flight to Honolulu three days before. My feeling at the time was that he hadn't really brought it back with us in mind, because he hadn't met us yet, and as a matter of fact, couldn't have even known that we would be moving in on that particular day. No. Rather, I think, he simply had brought it back to his wife Jane, (whom, in another one of my inelegant fantasies, I could envision him having had a fight with before departure), and upon his return Jane obligingly had worn it around her neck with nothing else on except a pair of spike heels (while they made up), and then, having grown tired of that, had stuffed it in the fridge where it remained in only slightly deteriorated condition for an occasional heady sniff, until we arrived and the inspiration hit Chet to offer it as a traditional symbol of greeting.

Nice as he is, Chet and I are not close. We are cordial, however, always waving at one another over the top of the hedge between our two properties, and shouting above the roar of either his or my power lawn mower, "How ya doin'?" I can't imagine us having much in common, unless, of course, I were to fly to Hawaii and he were to be piloting the plane, in which case a mutual interest in flight safety, I would hope, would unite us in a common bond.

He got his start as a pilot in the Air Force flying bombing missions over North Vietnam, a subject that Jane says to this day he won't talk about. While he was doing that I was living in Paris, France, not making the best use of my B.A. from Amherst, but spending a lot of time in French cafés assiduously avoiding the entreaties of my father to come back home and go to work. It was a period when I felt above any notions of going to work. With a few thousand dollars from cashed-in savings bonds that my parents had been amassing for me ever since my first birthday, I was able to spend a year in Paris, wearing a beret and smoking Gauloise cigarettes, absolutely convinced in my own mind that I was about to become a major young poet. In actuality, I hardly wrote anything, mostly sleeping until noon and spending the evenings with a coterie of like-minded American pals, all of us feeling invincible and superior while we sipped Pernod and watched the sidewalk crowds shuffle by. It was a time when my parents feared that I was going to renounce my American citizenship and become a French emigré, a notion I didn't totally discourage. I could have done anything, it seemed to me at the time. Certainly it did not seem at all necessary to form any long-range ideas to conform with anything my father had in mind. I actually did manage to complete a half dozen poems, sonnet exercises and rondels, which were no good at all, but were not so bad but what I was able to get them published in a mimeographed folio that about eight of us similar-minded non-working Americans living in the *sixième* put out (three times) that year (and only that year). It was called Odéon, and somewhere in the house I have several copies, the pages of which have long since turned brown and fall apart now when you open them. I have never published a poem since.

Entering my son's room is a little like entering a cavern deep below the surface of the sea. Certainly the blast of noise from within exerts a comparable increase in pressure on the ears. It is almost impossible to see anything without a torch, because my son has Scotch-taped cardboard posters over all the windows, and it is pitch black inside except for the red glow of a lamp with a blanket thrown over it and a candle that flickers regardless of the time of day or night in the top of a coffee can on a shelf. You reach the heart of this subaqueous domain by

11

penetrating layers of drapes that have been stapled to the ceiling, entrance slits at variance with a straight line, so that you have to zig to the left, then zag to the right, peeling aside one tie-dyed sheet after another before you are actually inside. There is an aroma suggestive of the sea, as well, somewhat like dried seaweed? Not, please, marijuana. *Raspberries*. My wife gave him a packet of raspberry-scented incense sticks for his last birthday, one of which is smoldering now in a dish on the floor next to the mattress he is sitting on cross-legged, Buddha-style. He looks up disinterestedly as he sees me, the way I remember that hoboes used to look up from their bonfires at new arrivals to their railroad camps in old Preston Sturges movies.

"Can you turn that thing down a little bit?" I cup hands to mouth so as to be heard.

Resignedly, and with no change of expression, he rolls over onto one hip, and reduces the volume. I have confirmed his negative expectations, as we both must have known I would.

"How ya doin'? Packed and ready?" It comes out with a false heartiness, the way I sound when I hail Chet Dowd over the hedge.

"Yeah." Like a stone dropping into a well.

"I'll help you take down the trunk."

"I can do it."

"I know you can, but I'll help you."

"Oh, all right."

He shuts off the stereo, and disconnects some wires. "Will my stereo ride all right?" he asks.

In response to even such a simple question as this, I experience a momentary elation; that he is actually seeking my opinion on something.

"We'll put a blanket under it. It'll be all right."

Manhandling his trunk to the top landing of the staircase that runs up along the side of the building, I can't imagine how he would have gotten it down by himself. But he is strong, and there is nothing that he is not willing to attempt. I have seen him stand on his hands, and do ten push-ups with his body pointing straight up at the sky.

I follow his lead in getting the trunk down, partly because somebody has to take charge, and he seems to assume the responsibility, and partly because I am not quite sure of just how to go about it, anyway. He seems to have a feeling for it. He takes the leather handle on his end in one hand, and I do the same, feeling that two hands would be better, but not wanting to appear less able than he. We start down the steps, with me below. Most of the weight is being supported by me, but actually, this is the easier end because at the top you have to bend over, holding yourself back while pulling up. But the weight of the thing is enormous, and I find myself being pushed hard against the cedar railing, which, in spite of the discomfort, I am grateful is there, since a crushed rib is certainly preferable to a broken collarbone as a result of a plunge fifteen feet over the side to the ground.

Unfortunately, before we can attain the bottom of the stairway the head of a minutely protruding nail catches in the fabric of my new gray flannel trousers, purchased just yesterday so as to impress the poohbahs at the fancy prep school we are to be driving to in a short while.

"Hold it! Wait!" The nail is caught, I can feel the tension around my thigh, but with no damage done as yet.

"I'm caught on a nail." I grunt it out, struggling to hold firm, and still. But the ineluctable momentum of the trunk forces me to stagger backward and downward to the next and bottom step. There is the sound of ripping flannel, and instantly the feel of cool air on groin.

"Oh, Jesus! Hold it, I said!" Immediately, by implication, throwing blame onto my son. A loathsome impulse; I am aware of it, even as I express it, which irrationally has the effect of further augmenting my rage.

"Let it down!" We are at the bottom of the stairway. Roughly I drop my end on the ground.

I look down at the front of my pants, at the rip running from the pocket to the top of the fly. "Agh-gh-gh-gh!" I rage at the world, which for the most part is blocked off by the back of my house from which my wife, brandishing a nail file in one hand, now emerges in a gray flannel suit that matches my pants.

"Need any help!" she calls.

"Agh-gh-gh-gh-gh!"

"What's the matter?"

"Look!" I scream. The ripped flap of flannel exposes powder blue boxer shorts matching the color of the glorious Indian Summer September sky.

"Oh, my goodness," my wife says, nail file frozen in midair. "Your new pants."

"This goddamn trunk!" My rage is so great I can only gurgle. The trunk is standing on its end on the ground, my son still up on the stairway, one hand resting on top of it, his expression now not quite so much indifferent as, rather, gleeful.

"They were brand new," my wife adds.

"I know what they were!" I realize that I must be bellowing,

14

because Chet Dowd's head appears over the top of the hedge by the side of the driveway.

I turn to my son. "Wipe that smirk off your face!" I manage a wave at Chet. "How ya doin', Chet?" And covering my wounded pants with both hands, I steal toward the house, three-quarter backside toward Chet, with this terrible inescapable image in my mind's eye that everything has turned out exactly as Frank, the Chief Executive Officer at my place of employment, might have predicted it would.

CHAPTER II

We are on our way, up the two-lane back road alongside the tree-shaded Housatonic River above Kent, driving toward the private boarding school that will cost me $11,000 a year for the next three years, where my son will be obliged to learn algebra, French, history, English, art and how to say, "Yes, sir," and look you in the eye, and not mumble, and wear gray flannel trousers and a blazer.

Good luck. I have changed my own trousers and am feeling better.

My daughter is with us. She who wears the pink frost lip gloss. She is wearing it today, I can see in the rearview mirror, in the hope, no doubt, that it will serve as an enticement to some poor lonely prep school freshman, already homesick and wandering forlornly about the greensward in front of the administration building.

My daughter is the one who should be going off to prep school. She approves of the whole idea, imagining it as a glamorous world of rich kids who go to Jamaica on spring vacations and Chamonix to ski at Christmas. She is half right. But since she is the one who gets all A's and B's, instead of C's and D's, she gets to stay home. There is no justice. Next year maybe, if Frank gives me a raise.

My daughter thinks I am funny, and when I stretch my neck slightly to catch a glimpse of her in the mirror, she has anticipated me, and stretches her neck exaggeratedly in mimicry. My son observes the interplay, but turns away from it, indicating that he is above this kind of silliness, although it was he who first initiated the routine just a year ago.

I don't concern myself about my daughter very much. This could be male chauvinism, I have considered it. But I think I am being truthful when I tell myself that I am leaving her alone because of a favorite maxim: If it works, don't fix it.

I would die for my daughter. Laura. Her bright and cheerful demeanor, her general easiness with the world, are precious to me, the most precious things in my life. Nevertheless, precisely for the reason that I feel so comfortable with her, I tend to take her for granted. The way, for example, that I take the country of Canada for granted, even though, I must say, Canada is not precious to me, nor would I die for Canada. Still, there is value in the image. As with Canada, I feel comfortable with her. I am glad she is nearby. Her reasonableness, her willingness to tolerate, even find amusement in, my assertiveness and dominance, I cherish, even though I spend very little time attending to her. I understand that she is a growing and vital young lady, with underlying growth pains that are her own, and separate, and having very little to do with me. Although she can be critical, she is not challenging me; she is not punishing me for my dominant position. She is not a *terrorist,* for Christ sake. She doesn't want my balls. She probably will be happy to grow up to marry someone just like me (What better choice could she make?) and lead a wonderful civilized and upwardly mobile existence, with our two families living in fairly close proximity, visiting occasionally on week-ends, respecting each other's privacy, and helping one another whenever possible. Is that too much to ask?

This is a point of view that any self-respecting radical feminist would probably label chauvinistic. Am I a male chauvinist? My wife is a pretty good judge of these matters. If I were to pose the question to her directly, in front of other people, she would feel obliged out of self-respect to say that I am; but with a look of amusement that, if not totally belying, would forgive all. If I should try to argue and defend, in front of other people, she would feel pressed to harden her position, and we would then find ourselves in a good half-hour heated exchange about who does the dishes, the cooking, the clean-ing, the breadwinning, etc., etc., ad nauseum, which would ony be half serious, and change nothing. It would, however, make us both feel, and the people with us feel, that we are engaged in serious conversation about serious contemporary matters.

In private, the subject, as such, would never come up. Rather, on some weekday night, as I most likely would be watching the seven o'clock news on the TV in our "country kitchen/family area" while my wife was preparing dinner, I might be made aware that she was setting dishes on the kitchen dining table with more than the usual gusto. This is a tacit signal of hers that she is pissed off, that she feels she is working too hard, doing all the dirty work, being taken advantage of, and is tired of being a house slave to the lord and master; that she has creative projects of her own, too, you know (photography), and she can't take photos, spend the whole day in the darkroom, and then do the laundry, the shopping, cook the dinner, and all the rest of it, while I sit with a drink in hand, eyes glued to the day's ravages on TV while she has to step around my feet to set the table.

Fifty years ago she would have borne it silently, or committed suicide. Today, they slam down dishes, and when you ask what the trouble is, because you can only ignore it up to a point without being ridiculous, she tells you. And then, if you give a damn, which I do, you get up off your ass, and try to help out. Sometimes it has already gone too far, and merely helping out for the moment will not do. In our case, invariably this means the initiation of a *discussion,* the initiating coming from me, since my wife, too angry by this point to discuss anything, would prefer to sulk for a day or two, which she knows is the worst punishment she can inflict on me. Passive-aggressive behavior they call it, I read that somewhere, probably in the dentist's waiting room. But from long experience, I have learned that she can stay angry only for a certain period of time; goodwill and patience and a willingness on my part to put up with her passive-aggressive abuse finally break through to the point. Male chauvinism then is discussed—not like at the party—the words themselves are never raised, and we forge out a new set of demands, most of them made on me. And, in truth, most of them reasonable. And thus, another new step forward for women has been taken. Until the next lapse, when we go through it again.

If I take my daughter for granted, as, I say, I take Canada, I would have to add that I take my wife for granted, too, but differently, probably more along the lines of the way I would take Great Britain. I don't mean to say that my wife is British, or in any way like the English. She is, in fact, descended from Austrian and Czechoslovak peasants. But I *think* of her the way

I think of Great Britain. It is as if none of us would be here without her. Annie. She is the mother country; handsome, though somewhat worn; just and fair in most matters (except when threatened directly, at which point her judgment is no better than anybody else's); dignified, to the extent that she does not involve herself in petty matters such as gossip and squabbles; and proud, deep-down proud, and therefore impossible to take advantage of for any extended period of time. She is patient, and somewhat wise, and when she tells you that you are wrong, and behaving badly, most of the time you had better listen. She is, in fact, my right arm, as the expression goes. And maybe more.

At this moment she is seated next to me in the front seat of the Pontiac, gazing placidly out the open window. It is a beautiful day, with sunshine glinting off the rippling current of the nearby Housatonic, even as it brightens fields of goldenrod spreading out in the distance, and throws deep dappled shadowing onto the highway through the overhanging trees. The foliage is just beginning to turn to fall coloring now, with small patches of brilliant red, orange and yellow showing up here and there amidst the thick summer greenery.

She is wearing a gray flannel suit, very stylish, with a beige blouse. Frank should see this family now. Me, in control, behind the wheel of the new Pontiac station wagon, wearing a regimental striped tie and a brown Harris tweed jacket (that is too damned hot). When I drive, I sit erect, so that all nearly six feet of me is on view to the passing world. Strong features, smooth-shaven, graying temples, with hair razor-trimmed stylishly long. My wife, trim and small, beside me. Daughter in the back seat, wide-eyed, alert, bright, in a summery dress, with black patent leather shoes, the heel raised about an inch.

21

And my son, peering out the tailgate, feet forcibly stuffed into real shoes (instead of sneakers), wearing corduroy pants, a shirt and *tie* (which I tied for him). A jacket that he has yet to put on is draped over the back seat. He has refused to wear it during our passage through any part of western Connecticut for fear that someone he knows might see him.

For sure, the gang he has begun to hang out with back home would not win any sartorial awards. A motley bunch, who do not come to the house, but, rather, loiter about in the nearby vicinity of the Grand Union shopping center. These are kids of high school age, some still in school, some who have dropped out, who gather each afternoon, rain or shine, and mill about aimlessly and sort of camp out on the edge of the parking lot under the trees near the town public park. When you park your car to do your shopping you see them in the shadows imbibing from bottles barely concealed in paper bags, and generally acting like Bowery bums. My son will not, or cannot, explain what he sees in these kids, but there is no doubt that there is an attraction to them. And we are scared shitless.

Dressed somewhat like rebels of the '60s, from my distant vantage point they seem to be the last remnants of that tattered rebellious army of radical hippies, but arrayed not so much now against any cultural organizations or systems of life, as against life itself. I cannot be sure, but from what I can gather from my son's new empathetic feelings toward them, they seem to have no convictions about anything, except sadness, and death. Images of the human skull dominate their drawings, their music, and probably their dreams. A straw of hope is that their raggle-taggle performance in the parking lot could be a last desperate, if pathetic, effort to act out their sadness in life rather than to succumb to suicidal impulses as so many of their more straightlaced contemporaries seem to be doing. What is the rate of suicide among the young? It seems to be rising every year to alarming proportions. Or is that just another media hype? I know that my son is sad; that in his sadness he has turned from his cheerful sister with whom he was always so very close, and from us, as if whatever cheerfulness we manage now to summon up and project to the world is a fraud, and unworthy of his attention, not to mention his love.

This is why we have made the decision to send our son to this costly school that we are now approaching from the long gracefully winding gravel driveway toward the brick and white Georgian administration building at the top of the slope—not for him to develop expensive spring vacation travel habits, nor even to wear that goddamn blazer thrown over the back seat with such deliberate carelessness (which I am rather pleased with myself for not having commented on), but to—*please, dear God*—enable him to go on and see some glimmer of hope—even if he has to break his heart ultimately in a vain struggle to make it come out right and human in the end. That's all we want, that he should hope, and strive, and survive. And therein perhaps is true dignity. Who knows?

There is a group of what I suppose are upper classmen awaiting our arrival outside the dorm entrance where my son is to live. My heart gives a joyful thump as they greet us with smiles and firm handshakes, and with offers to help lug my son's gear up to the second floor of the building. They are the official greeters, and I note sneakily from a distance that they are engaged in easy exchanges of information with my son about his stereo, his BMX stunt bicycle, his set of barbells and weights, his skis and other teen-age paraphernalia that I had thought would be of no interest to anyone except the thugs in the Grand Union parking lot. (Where are the tennis racquets of yesteryear? The stacks of Fitzgerald and Hemingway books? At least *Catcher in the Rye,* for Christ sake?)

I *love* the roommate they have picked for my son, a nerd if ever there was one. Shy, awkward, wearing glasses, and in no way ever a candidate for admission to the parking lot fraternity. The school has matched sophomore roommates by computer (they are very proud to disclose to us), and here we have my son, the urban guerrilla terrorist, with Mr. Nerd. Thank God for computers and the errors that they are constantly spewing forth.

But, of course, a dark cloud quickly scuds across the horizon. My daughter, with the finely attuned antennae of a modern teen-ager herself, immediately notes that the new boy has several faded jean jackets on hooks in the closet, a suitcase full of tie-dyed shirts, a collection of rock music tapes even more outrageous than my son's ("Hey, all right!" she exclaims. Which leads me to begin to wonder if she is going to turn on us, too), and an electric fan.

"So, what's the deal about the fan?" I ask.

My daughter looks back at me with an expression of disbelief and something approaching contempt. For the first time in her life, I notice an ugly maturity is beginning to creep into her face. "Come on, Dad. That's to blow smoke out of the room."

"Smoke?! What do you mean, smoke?" I am all for going immediately to the headmaster, but my wife restrains me with the reassurance that she has already met the roommate's mother who has relayed the information that her son suffers from asthma and hay fever. The fan is for the purpose of blowing out the window pollen seeds of goldenrod that abound in these parts.

"Yeah, Dad," my daugher says. "Don't worry so much."

"Don't tell me not to worry," I snap at her. But almost immediately I realize that I am probably overreacting, and I manage to pull myself into a state resembling composure again. "I'm sorry, honey. You're right. I'm a worry wart."

We have transported everything up to my son's room. Gasping slightly from the effort, I stand for a moment and look about. It is a bleak little cell. One small window. A bunk bed against one wall. Two square frame desks with straight-backed chairs. No rug. No drapes. No pictures on the wall. Only that goddamn fan on one of the two identical bureau dressers.

I put on my most jovial smile, and stick out a paw at my son. It is time to go. He takes my hand, and then looking up at me from under the mop of black hair that has fallen across his eyes, he smiles at me. For the first time in weeks. Maybe months. Instantly I feel my face falling apart, and involuntarily I let out a ridiculous indeterminate noise, and throw both arms about his shoulders. His own arms go about my waist. Only for a moment, and then we break.

"Keep your nose clean," I say.

His mother takes both of his elbows in her hands, and draws him to her for a kiss on the mouth. He voluntarily hugs her. Encouraged, his sister goes for a kiss, too, but is repulsed with a stiff arm and a cry, "No way!" It comes out in a high little boy squeak which his voice occasionally still slips into, and it is funny enough so that even he laughs, and my daughter goes in for another try, giggling, but gets nowhere. But it doesn't matter, because he is giggling with her, and she couldn't have asked for more.

New kids from down the hall have moved into the doorway to check out my son. Quickly we slip through them to give them their shot.

"'Bye, hon," his mother says.

"So long," he says, and offers a small cheery wave.

In the station wagon on the way down the long winding gravel driveway, past other station wagons and sedans parked alongside on the grass, our daughter, I observe in the rear view mirror, is looking back.

"It's nice," she muses approvingly.

Out of the corner of my eye I glance over at my wife. She is not looking back. She is directing her eyes straight ahead at the road, as I do now, too.

CHAPTER III

Monday morning, 7:45, and a long way away from the events of yesterday and the trip up to my son's boarding school. It promises to be another lovely Indian Summer September day, as I look out at the tarmac landing strip at La Guardia airport through a window of the Boeing 747 in which I am seated, next to a heavily made-up beefy-faced lady who is wearing what looks like a red fright wig and glasses with ribbon dangling from the temples. She is chewing on and periodically snapping an enormous cud of Juicy Fruit gum (I can tell from the smell that it is Juicy Fruit) and chatting gaily with her husband seated on the other side of her, a diminutive man who appears to be about half her size, who is wearing a suit that is too large for him and whose mostly balding head is afflicted with sores. He talks to her across the back of his hand, in a hoarse whisper, as though he might have been gassed in a war. We are all waiting to take off for Las Vegas, my two traveling companions looking forward to five days of gambling, it turns out, and I to two days of working at a convention that my company—using the word "my" loosely, of course—is participating in out there at the Las Vegas Convention Center.

"Welcome aboard flight 516 direct to Las Vegas, ladies and gentleman," comes a comforting familiar voice over the loud speaker. "I'm Captain Dowd"—oh, my God!—"and our flight crew today consists of Second Captain Irwin Brown and Flight Engineer Jamie Hopewell. The bad news, folks, is we've got a few fellas ahead of us this morning—about 18—so it'll be a little while before we get off the ground. I can only suggest, just sit back and relax, and we should be cleared for departure in about 36 minutes."

I'm ravenously hungry, having gotten out of bed at 4:30 this morning and skipped even coffee to catch the 5:30 limo to La Guardia, (I could have ridden in with Chet in his Jeep Wagoneer), so as to get to the airport one hour ahead of the scheduled departure of flight 516, which according to the travel bureau itinerary in my pocket promises to serve a "full breakfast." I wouldn't mind catching a bit more sleep while we wait, but sleep is out of the question, since the entire cabin of the plane is filled with shouting revellers on some kind of club excursion to Caesar's Palace, and my adjacent traveling companion knows them all, and between snaps of her gum, keeps up a regular barrage of witticisms flying across my head.

"Aggie! Aggie! Better wawdjout! I'll tell Augie!" Which provokes a crescendo of laughter, rejoined by, "Nevuh mind! How abowjew?"

Talk about dignity, in the presence of this kind of raucousness, invariably I find myself adopting the mannerisms and demeanor of the Prime Minister of England. But I have no luck. I seem to be one of those people who, when I withdraw into frosty isolation from others, only provoke them into peering intently into my face, garlic breath hot on my eyeballs, as if to check out if I am all right, or perhaps to see if there is a real person present inside the crusty shell.

"Hiya," says the beefy lady next to me. "Goyna Vegas?"

"I beg your pardon." Neville Chamberlain without the umbrella.

Undaunted, she pushes right on. "Me and Aldo gowout coupla timesa year."

"I see."

"We ewjly make enough to payfa the trip and a coupla weeks in Hawaii."

"You *do?*"

I'm sitting here, feeling smug and superior, on my way to this terrible business convention, while this lady next to me is whooping and hollering with her friends, and having the best time of her life, and will continue to have a great time for another five days, before returning home with all her expenses paid and enough extra change in her pockets to go off with Aldo for two more weeks to Hawaii. If Chet Dowd loses control of the plane and we go down over Indianapolis, who has had the better life—me in my Brooks Brothers flannels and navy blazer and dignified manner, or Mrs. Gumsnap and Aldo and their crowd who are right now shouting and twisting and turning like dervishes and tormenting me with tantalizing stories of riches they expect to make beyond imagining?

"How the hell doya do that?" I ask her, dropping the British accent.

"Aldo shoots craps. I play poker. We alwuz win."

"Geez, no kiddin'."

And now, pals until at least when the plane gets up and then down, we talk. Or rather, she does. I am fascinated. Aldo was in the wholesale fruit and vegetable business in Hunt's Point market for fifteen years until he hurt his back. Now he gets workman's compensation, and plays the horses, and makes a wonderful living.

Aldo takes an interest in the conversation, leaning across his wife's lap to tell me in a hoarse whisper about a "nag" that is running in the seventh at Belmont this afternoon, and he has $15,000 on him. If I want to do myself a favor, he tells me, when we get to Vegas I should put a bundle on the nose of this horse, Raggedy Ann, because I'll be able to retire when he comes in first. Aldo was not gassed, I don't think. He simply talks like a godfather. I could tell him, I suppose, that whatever extra funds I have are tied up right now in my son's education, but even if I had the money, I wouldn't bet it, because I'd lose. He's lucky I'm not betting on his horse.

Aldo's wife is Loretta—last name, Bellagamba. They live in Co-op City and have a terrace with a wonderful view of the South Bronx, which from a distance, they tell me, looks like Venice, figure that, and they raised three sons in their apartment, which has four rooms, including kitchen and living room. One son is a cameraman with NBC News. "Every Friday, they run the names of the crew at the end of the show," Loretta tells me. And, you know, I'll probably look for the name Bellagamba the next time I am in my country kitchen at home and watching the six o'clock news while my wife walks around my feet setting the kitchen dining table.

Another son, Loretta tells me, is an accountant, with De-Loitte, Haskins & Sells (my company's accounting firm), and the youngest son, Tommy, now twenty, Aldo doesn't want her to talk about ("Nevva minedat," he whispers). But obviously Tommy is Loretta's favorite, and she has to tell all. He's been convicted of car theft, and he takes drugs, and Aldo threw him out of the house. ("Wha wudjew do?" he asks me), and he's the "smottest one a duh treeya dem." And they don't even know where he is right now. Having divested herself of this enor-

30

mous grievous burden, Tommy's mother can't talk about it anymore now, as she is about to cry, and she looks over my head for Aggie or Augie, or somebody to hurl an insult at that will get the laughter rolling again, and I don't know—welcome to the club, folks. She bears this enormous burden that is eating her heart out with such great good cheerfulness, who the hell would dare argue that with all of her brassiness she isn't the most dignified person aboard the plane?

The thirty-six minutes stretches out to 50, with Chet Dowd coming on every five minutes or so, and the stewardesses cheerfully doing their part to reassure us of how safe it is to fly by reminding us to buckle up our seat belts, and read the emergency procedure card in the pocket of the seat in front of us, and note the location of the emergency exits, as well as the instructions on how to inflate our life preservers, and how to put on our oxygen masks "in the unlikely event" that we should need to. Loretta's stories make the time pass quickly, and suddenly we are "next in line and cleared for departure, folks."

Up, up, and away. Chet noses us up beautifully over La Guardia, with the familiar thrill in the pit of the stomach as the rear of the plane humps up off the ground, and the clinger sounds and the "Fasten Seat Belt" sign goes off, and the cabin fills with the smell of hot coffee, and while Loretta and Aldo practice blackjack on the service table in front of them, I feel myself psyching up for the three days ahead.

This is an important trip for me. My company is a major manufacturer and supplier of prosthetic devices, and with the recent proliferation of internal plastic parts, such as artificial hearts, kidneys, breasts, sexual transplant organs, etc., business is thrumming. No part of the human body is off limits to us, and we have a whole division devoted just to Research and

31

Development located in Cologne, Germany. The company actually is German, and our U.S. group, as they call us, is primarily a sales and marketing organization that the Krauts, as we call them, hope someday will become the largest group company in the world, and that means the largest of thirty-three, including Zambia.

The company is called Pro-Tec, which can sound a little bit like a prophylactic to some Americans, but the Germans don't realize that, and none of the Americans, including Frank, has ever had the temerity to point it out to them. Tec, for technology, is a sound that sends our parent company directors into paroxyms of delight. Anyway, it would be too late to change the name now, as we are well known in medical circles, and have spent a lot of time and money building up our name. We do get phone inquiries from porno suppliers and distributors wanting to handle our line, but we have a pretty divorcée at the switchboard who has gotten over her initial embarrassment and is quite hard-nosed now about heading these calls off and setting the callers straight.

As director of advertising and public relations, I am responsible for expending a little more than $1 million annually in advertising to a variety of trade publications such as *Precision Prosthetics, Prosthetic Technology,* and *The American Review of Prosthetic Devices.* Talk about wild reading. Because it's my job to know what's happening in the world of prosthetic devices, I feel obligated to at least thumb through these magazines every month when they appear. When I am particularly keyed up at night and feel that I will not be able to get to sleep easily, I settle down with the *American Review* into my Air-Flow recliner in my den/office off the living room, and I can expect to be asleep within ten minutes.

In addition to working with an advertising agency in the preparation of and placement of ads, my responsibilities include setting up publicity arrangements for a variety of trade show events that take place every year, the largest one of them all occurring every two years, and that being the International Prosthetics & Surgical Equipment Exposition at Las Vegas, which is what I am heading toward now.

Pro-Tec is introducing a new product at the Vegas Show this year that the Krauts believe is ten years ahead of anybody else and that they hope will capture the major share of market in prosthetic devices world-wide. It is a plastic hand that works chemically, instead of mechanically. Basically, the way I describe it to the editors whom I take to lunch is that it is a plasticized molded hand constructed on the inside with pockets of absorbent chemical materials (the composition of which is unimportant) that contract and expand instantaneously in various desirable ways when subjected to electrical charges triggered by nerve impulses. It is, indeed, an incredible breakthrough in prosthetic devices.

The Krauts, again with unusual sensitivity to the nuances of the English language, have named their new artificial appendage the "Hand-Arbiter," from the German *arbeiter* for work, or job, which translates loosely into English, if you want to think about it, as hand-job. This is what everybody calls it at Pro-Tec U.S.A. Everybody except Frank.

Chet sets the Boeing 747 down nicely on the ground at McCarran International, and while we wait for our luggage at one of the carousels, Loretta hits the silver dollar jackpot at one of the nearby slot machines, and Aldo returns grinning from one of the pay phones where he has just placed a credit card long distance call.

We share a cab together to Caesar's Palace, Aldo insisting on paying the fare, and giving the driver a $10 tip. When we arrive at the entrance, the doorman greets the Bellagambas by name and with effusive respect, snapping his fingers for not one, but two bellhops to carry their bags, one of whom I am able finally to browbeat into carrying my bags too, by screaming at him that I am a member of the Bellagamba party.

Inside the lobby the Bellagambas and I part company with a mutual promise to get together for drinks before the next three days are out.

I have never been here before. After I am registered, another bellhop guides me through a seemingly endless maze of brightly illuminated slot machines to what I take to be the opposite far side of the hotel, at which point we go back out into the bright sun again and down some steps and then up to another level overlooking a vast open area with pool and poolside bar, continuing our journey back inside another wing of the building, then down a hall to an elevator and up finally to my room. I have the feeling I may never be able to find my way back to the lobby without help.

The room itself is about three times the size of the bedroom in our home, with a king-size bed on a raised platform, and mirrors on the ceiling overhead. The mirrors are intended to enhance Bacchanalian nights, but are largely wasted on me, since I tend to prefer the lights off, or at least dimmed when I go for it, which I do not expect to do, anyway, during the term of my visit here.

Anyway, it's good to be safely in Las Vegas at twelve noon local time. I am due to attend shortly a meeting at Pro-Tec's Convention Center exhibit area to go over last-minute plans prior to tomorrow's convention opening. This is the biggest show of its kind for the prosthetics industry, and everybody who is anybody is here. Which explains why the Krauts have spent $1 million on the Pro-Tec exhibit, a display area so large they are not able to fit it inside the Convention Center. Instead, we are to be located outside, directly in front of the entrance to the hall. According to the detailed plans that I have seen, our display is laid out in the form of a carpeted mall bordered by individual stalls to be manned by experts (our sales force) hawking mechanical legs, hands, glass eyes, a working plastic heart (connected to a model of a human circulatory system), and an area devoted to sex change devices, including things I don't even want to think about made of goat chamois. At the end of the mall, rising up above it and looming over it somewhat like the Taj Mahal, or at least like a sultan's summer palace, there is to be an air-conditioned red-and-white striped circus tent, pennants flying, the interior of which will include an open bar, free snack and sandwich service, plus a complex of private administration offices, rest rooms, telephones, a closed circuit TV room, an executive conference room, and a large center tiled piazza area with tables and chairs for enjoying the refreshments in air-conditioned splendor while our sales force pitches prospective customers on our lines of products.

It is in this center hall area where tomorrow we will hold a press conference at noon at which time it will be my responsibility to introduce the Hand-Arbiter to eighteen editors from the various trade publications that are most important to us. I know all of the editors on a first-name basis, and have invited them to drop by for a beer and a sandwich at noon and to get a

first-hand look-see at what we think is the single most signifi-
cant breakthrough in the prosthetics industry in the past forty
years. Inventor of the Hand-Arbiter, Dr. Wolfgang Feigenweiser, who got his early on-the-job training in prosthetics
during and immediately after World War II, will be present to
answer any questions. I can count on these editors showing up,
because they know from past years' experience that our air-
conditioned tent is the most comfortable place at the convention where they can sit down and get a free lunch, and I
like to think they trust me enough so that when I tell them I
have an important story for them, they will take note. Just in
case, I told them that if they didn't show I'd be goddamned if
they'd ever again get an advertisement placed in their magazine from Pro-Tec.

So I'm feeling fairly relaxed in my seraglio here at Caesar's
Palace, freshening up with that endocrine soap they supply,
when suddenly I am surprised by the ringing of my telephone.
And I'm even more surprised after I pick up to hear the raspy
Jersey intonations of Aldo Bellagamba, whom I left no more
than twenty minutes ago (about the length of time it
took the bellhop and me to move our caravan cross-country to
the room). Is it possible he has another tip on a horse?

"Where are yuh?" he demands, right off the bat.

"What do you mean, where am I? I'm right here."

"Well, we been waitin' an hour."

"What are you, drunk?"

"Hey, hey. Dere yuh go again. Ya don't loin, doya?"

"Is this Al?"

"Dis is Frank."

"Frank?! Oh, Frank! Why didn't you say so?"

"Yuh alwuz gotta come up wi' duh smot remok, doncha?"

"Frank, I didn't know it was you. I thought it was one of those smooth insurance fellows I met on the plane."

"We're waitin ta go ovuh you pot a duh show."

"My what?" He's hard to understand sometimes.

"Hey, lissen, willya, I don' ha' time ta say evrytin' twice."

"Yes, Frank. Sorry. I'll be right over. Don't worry about the press conference, though. Everything's all set."

"Dat's wutchew tink. Dey gotta few idees dey wantcha t'add."

"*Who's* got a few ideas? Everything's all set, Frank."

"Seeya in a coupla minutes." And he hangs up, which I take to mean that the conversation is over.

I make it down to the outdoor pool area, and then by asking here and there am able to find my way back to the lobby. At the front door they still think I am a member of the Bellagamba party, so I have no trouble getting a cab, and in ten minutes I am at the front of our Pro-Tec exhibit area at the Convention Center, which I find easily, because the Krauts have rigged up a barrage balloon directly overhead that looks like a giant sausage and says PRO-TEC on both sides.

Not quite sprinting, but moving briskly down the center mall through the bazaar of exhibits on either side, I catch glimpses out of the corner of my eyes of various of my colleagues from our corporate offices already acclimatizing themselves to their respective stalls where they will be hawking their wares tomorrow. What is most incredible is that together they look like an assemblage of prep school freshmen, having been fitted out to a man in identical uniforms of gray flannel trousers, navy blazers with brass buttons, Oxford button-down shirts and regimental ties striped with Pro-Tec's official colors, red black and gold, the same colors, coincidentally, of the

Third Reich. Once upon a time, and not so terribly long ago either, you had to be recommended by three generations of yachting club members before you would dare presume to wear an outfit like the one these salesmen, and I, are all wearing now.

Frank, also in flannels and blazer, is seated on a couch in the executive administration office, his feet up and resting proprietarily on a coffee table. In his gold-chained loafers, he looks like a manager of a cut-rate shoe store.

" 'Sabout time," he says.

He is faced by others seated in easy chairs, my colleagues and peers from head office whom I know and, in fact, work with on a daily basis, and a couple of Germans whom I don't know.

Nobody introduces anybody, but I recognize from photos that I have seen of him that the old German, the only one not in gray flannels and blazer, is Dr. Wolfgang Feigenweiser himself, and he, indeed, rises to introduce himself. We shake hands, and immediately I am aware that I am gripping my first fully connected and functioning Hand-Arbiter. Although it is the closest thing to a real hand that man has yet to devise, it feels like a palmful of knockwurst, and it responds to my clasp about a second and a half late, and when I unclasp, I am not immediately reassured that it is going to let go. But it does. Grasping a Hand-Arbiter in the flesh, so to speak, is different from seeing one in a box, which has been my only contact with one up to now. Dr. Feigenweiser grins, presenting a hideous leer in which one side of his mouth turns up while the other side implodes downward. He fastens one steady eye on me through amber-tinted glass. The other eye I cannot see because the lens, though not amber, is frosted over. I notice that he limps slightly when he steps toward me, and before sitting down, gives the thigh of his left leg a thump with his good hand, that is, the one that is not rubber. At least, I assume it's not rubber.

"Ach, so," Feigenweiser says. "You vill ingwoduce Hand-Arbeiter (He uses the German pronunciation) to ze pwess, no?"

"Yes," I say.

"Gut. Ve haf al-zo zum ideas."

Seated next to Dr. Feigenweiser is a muscular looking lady of about forty in a black pants suit and regimental necktie, who introduces herself as Dr. Feigenweiser's assistant, Fraulein Shatsie, Shatsie being either her first or her last name, but in any case, not connected to any other. She does not smile. Except for a heavy eyeliner, she wears no make-up. There is a cigar next to a fountain pen sticking out of her jacket hanky pocket.

The others in the room are all well-known to me, my colleagues and peers, first, Morrie Glick, Director of Marketing, whom I work with closest back at Head Office; Morrie's secretary/assistant Diana Payne-Pignatelli; and Tony Passanante, National Sales Manager. I like these people. Correction: I like both of the men, each of whom loathes the other; I think they both like me, or at least, do not have an outright aversion to me. The woman, Diana Payne-Pignatelli, I cannot stand even to be in the same room with for more than a few minutes at a time, but this is right in the mainstream of thinking at Pro-Tec Head office, where she is the one person most despised by every level of employee from mailroom clerk to field district managers, except by Morrie who sleeps with her as often as he can, that is, whenever he can get her out of town and away from her husband, whom Morrie assures me also likes her. She is shapely, and not bad looking, if the expresson of self-importance on her face that contracts her forehead into a perpetual knotted frown and squeezes her lips up into something like a Hershey's kiss doesn't turn your stomach. She is here because she is in charge of hotel room arrangements for Pro-Tec personnel attending the show, plus ticket reservations for any Vegas shows that Pro-Tec sales people will be inviting prospective customers to all week. Anyone who wants a bed to sleep in, or tickets to any show worth going to must report to Miss Piggy, as the salesmen refer to her. She can put you either in a laundry closet or in the Augustan suite, depending on her perception of your importance in the company. She has Frank in a penthouse up on the top floor of Caesar's, and Morrie has a suite on the floor below, adjoining her own room.

The group has been waiting for me, because Dr. Feigenweiser, concerned lest his invention not receive the kind of auspicious press introduction tomorrow that it deserves, has arranged for a few embellishments to ensure its success. First of all, he has prepared a few remarks of his own that he would like to distribute to the assembled editors. He produces a typewritten treatise four pages long, single-spaced, describing in what the Americans at Pro-Tec refer to as Germlish (a bad English translation of an original German text), a history of the development of the Hand-Arbiter artificial hand.

"No one believed at first that I would be able ever to develop an artifical digital appendage that would raise the state of the art to new heights never before imagined," it starts out. Looking it over, my feeling is that it is worthless from a publicity point of view. But I am thoroughly accustomed to corporate ego stroking; and after all, the guy is a creative genius, in a way; so it doesn't really bother me that his treatise should be included in the press packet that we will distribute to our editor guests tomorrow at the press introduction.

"I vill read it und anzwer any quvestions," Dr. Feigenweiser states.

"What's that? Excuse me, doctor. You want to *read* this?"

"Ja. It's wary emportant zet zey untershtand vhat ve are trywing to do by vay of backgwound."

"It's really good stuff, Doctor, but it will take about twenty minutes to read this."

"Tventy-fife."

"Do you think that's a good idea?"

"Ve did it in Homburg, und zey loved it."

Fraulein Shatsie nods her head vigorously in confirmation.

I look over at Frank to see where the strength is going to come from. Frank is listening with what I can only assume is a dignified expression, his head slightly cocked to one side, like the attentive pooch on old Victor record albums. No help from his corner.

Morrie Glick is actually beaming, showing his enthusiasm for the idea, spittle glistening on his teeth. I don't know why I even bother to look at Morrie. I know him well enough to be certain, in advance, that he will never disagree with a Kraut, no matter what he thinks. Years ago Morrie confided to me after a couple of martinis together somewhere on the road that his greatest worry in life was that "the Nazi pricks," his term for our employers, would get it into their heads somehow that he is Jewish, thus, in his view, ruining his chances for advancement within the company. In point of fact, Morrie is not Jewish, and has not been Jewish for twenty years, ever since he

41

joined the Baptist church at the time when he changed his career from tummeler in the borscht belt to go into marketing. Nevertheless, whenever he is in the presence of the Krauts he falls all over himself to be ingratiating. He has given me strict instructions that in the internal Pro-Tec house organ that I am responsible for editing, his name should always appear as Morris, and not Morrie, the latter being a nickname which he feels is undignified. My own feeling is that he would do himself more good with the Krauts by standing up straight to them, and I have told him so, and he has even agreed with me, but the minute a German walks into the room he starts salivating. Diana, who has no firm opinions of her own on anything, except that her progress within the company is secure as long as Morrie has her under his wing, or whatever, takes her lead from him now, and still keeping the Hershey kiss look on her lips, manages to compress her cheeks into an approving simper.

Tony Passanante, I can tell, agrees with me, but since Tony thinks that all publicity and communications are a lot of shit anyway, he simply looks stony-faced at a fingernail on his left hand which he slowly brings up to his front incisors for a clipping, squinting his eyes tightly shut the minute I look in his direction.

"Tell him the best part, Dr. Feigenweiser," says Morrie, sitting up with paws crooked.

"Ja. I vuz chust going to," Feigenweiser snaps, looking annoyed at Morrie. Morrie's smile transmogrifies into a wince. "Chentlemens! Mein Herren!" Feigenweiser calls out, raising the splayed rubber fingers of his hand-job over his head and waving it about. "Kommen sie herein!"

42

And the door to the room opens, and in file ten total strangers, all non-English speaking Germans, all in identical navy blazers and neckties, who move about the room, clicking their heels and extending to all present a rubber hand of greeting.

"Ve flew zem in last night," Dr. Feigenweiser says, beaming with pride, "mit zer idea of placing zem among ze pwess vhen ve ingwoduce Hand-Arbeiter. At zer end, zey vill all shake hands mit zer pwess people, und zey vill first-hand zee for zemselves zer miracle of modern zi-enz."

"Isn't that great!" Morrie Glick puts in.

All eyes are on me. I am looking around the room at the one-handed models flown over from Germany, or more likely from Tobruk, Africa. They look like a terrorist squad masquerading as a soccer team sent out by the French Foreign Legion.

"Do you think it might be overdoing things a bit?" I ask. But there is no heart in it. The Krauts have put up a million bucks to set up this show, and they will have their way. I flash Dr. Feigenweiser what I hope is a winning smile, taking my lead from Morrie's expression.

"Anytin' else?" Frank is on his feet, his eyes from behind the horn-rimmed glasses quickly scanning our faces. Everybody, on cue as though drilled in a Greek chorus, shakes his head dolorously. Frank stretches his arms over his head, utters a loud and somewhat agonized groan of release, and walks out the door.

Everyone looks questioningly at one another, as if not certain yet whether or not the meeting is over. But it is; at least, if Frank's departure is in keeping with the way he customarily ends all of his meetings. Tony Passanante breaks the spell of post-meeting stasis, with a grin at me, and a loud-voice greeting.

"Brock, you hot shit. How the hell are ya?" This is intended not so much really as a greeting as a way to antagonize Diana who has let it be known on numerous occasions that she objects strenuously to male profanity, particularly from Tony.

I sidle over to Passanante, and in a somewhat lower tone, growl at him, "Thanks for backing me up on the Kraut soccer team, you prick."

Tony bursts into a roar of laughter. "You noticed?"

Dr. Feigenweiser is huddled with Shatsie and the ten Germans on the other side of the room, speaking in muted German. The twelve of them, all looking over at us, suddenly break into laughter, at the same time, to a man (including Shatsie) blushing. We all smile back good-naturedly. Morrie actually waves.

"What are they saying, Morrie?" Tony asks, gibing.

"Nazi pricks," Morrie says, waving again and broadening his grin.

The Nazi pricks file out of the room, Shatsie following after them, like a prison matron. Dr. Feigenweiser approaches, wearing his Halloween leer. "Hello zere," he says cheerily. "Zey vere zaying zey are looking vorvart to ze pwess meeting tomowwow."

"Do you like speaking in front of large groups of press people, Dr. Feigenweiser?" I ask him. It occurs to me as a last resort that maybe I can plant a few seeds of stage fright to make him change his mind.

"I zink id vill eggsplain zings to zem bedder."

It will drive them screaming from the air-conditioned splendor and comfort of our circus tent back into the blast furnace of the Las Vegas desert.

"Yes, probably," I say.

Feigenweiser nods politely and militarily at Morrie and Tony, then reaches for Diana's hand, which reflexively and instantaneously she draws back behind her, possibly thinking he has in mind stealing her ring, before she recovers and yields it up for a Continental kiss, at the moment of which, her eyes, in a contraction of royalist ecstasy, roll inward toward the point of her lips.

"C'mere, Brock," Tony Passanante says, He draws me apart from Morrie and Diana. "You wanna get in the raffle?"

"What raffle?"

"For a blow job. Ten bucks. I got ten guys already. I need another five."

Actually, no, I don't really want to win a blow job in a raffle. Back home I don't even enter Junior Chamber of Commerce raffles to win a Cadillac.

"Did you ask Morrie?" This is simply a stall while I try to come up with a diplomatic way of declining. It is important that I remain on the right side of Tony, who, in his way, is a power at Pro-Tec.

"Are you kiddin'? He's got Miss Piggy. Come on, kick in."

Tony has little patience with demurring, which is probably why his sales force succeeded in bringing in over $100 million in orders for prosthetic devices last year.

"A lousy ten bucks, Brock. You a white man, or what?"

Since I have never won anything in my life, I figure, What the hell. Ten bucks for goodwill.

"You got change for a twenty?"

"Hell, no," he says. "Take two."

45

"*One,* Tony. Gimme ten bucks back." A man's dignity demands that he draw a line somewhere.

Tony reaches in his pocket and pulls out an enormous roll of ten dollar bills. He isn't kidding; he's been hustling.

Morrie sidles up to us. "What're you guys up to?"

"Tell you later," says Tony, looking at me, and winking. I can only cast a bleak smile at Morrie.

"Diana's got a block of tickets to Wayne Newton," Morrie says. We're taking Feigenweiser and the Krauts. You guys want to go?"

"Wayne Newton?" says Tony. "Sure. I'll go."

I only know of Wayne Newton by reputation, but I tend to rate him on about the same level as the prize in Tony's raffle, though perhaps this is unfair. Diana sashays over, brimming with largesse.

"Make up your mind, fellows, because Wayne Newton tickets are in big demand."

I am tempted to inquire by whom, but instead, I say, "Sounds great, Diana. Thanks." Aside from arranging for rooms at conventions, Diana derives her power from her close relationship with Morrie into whose ear I can just imagine her whispering in the darkest moments of the night, things like, "Do you really think Brock knows what he's doing with his ads?" Since Morrie can do as much for or against my advertising programs as Tony, I make it a point always of treating Diana with the utmost respect. She likes to have doors opened for her, for example, which I always beat everybody else out of the way to do, unless Morrie happens to be there first, in which case I yield to his *droit de seigneur.*

"You're welcome," she says, and reaches in her handbag and

pulls out a ticket each for Tony and me. "Don't lose them," she says. "They can't be replaced."

Obediently, I put mine in my wallet right in front of her where she can see I'm taking good care of it.

She pirouettes, and gives a little flutter of her fingers over her shoulder. "'Bye," she says. "See youse at the show." Despite a daily continuing heroic effort on Diana's part to cover the remaining traces of an accent acquired from her early childhood upbringing in Hoboken, she does occasionally slip up.

And we file out of the room together, the others to take a taxi back to Caesar's Palace, I to the Yellow Pages and thence to a local Print-Qwik Shop to get the good doctor's background treatise photocopied for the press conference tomorrow, and then back to Caesar's Palace in time for a bite to eat in my room and to make ready for Wayne Newton.

CHAPTER IV

At nine o'clock in the evening I meet Morrie, Diana, and the others in the lobby of Caesar's Palace at the base of an ornate and thickly carpeted stairway leading up to the grand ballroom where Wayne Newton "and company" are appearing in an "all-star revue."

The lobby is jam-packed with hotel guest gawkers jostling against slot machine players and gamblers and cocktail wait-resses in off-the-shoulder miniskirt togas, the latter weaving in amongst us with trays of free drinks. In the background, seemingly penned against the wall by a velvet rope, is a restless raggedy line of people extending all the way up the staircase and back down into the lobby and out of sight around a corner, as far back, it would seem, as Omaha.

Diana is wearing an off-the-shoulder toga gown herself, except hers reaches to the floor, and I must say, until I catch a glimpse of the feral expression on her face, for a moment I can see why Morrie is crazy about her.

Morrie, in keeping with the festiveness of the occasion, has exchanged his gray flannels for white flannels and is wearing an open collar pink silk shirt with a gold chain around his neck. Morrie is not tall, but stands a bit higher in high gloss black plastic elevator shoes. The pink shirt, which is beautiful, does

49

clash, however, with the orange tint of his hair which he grows long near his left ear and layers in strands over his bald spot. Tony Passanante wears an Izod Kelly green polo shirt, and carries a double knit jacket over one arm, in case it is required that it be worn to hear Wayne Newton.

Dr. Feigenweiser and I are the only ones dressed inappropriately for the occasion, he in the same tired business suit he was wearing during the afternoon, and I, like the ten Kraut terrorists who are huddled nearby with Shatsie, in the same soccer team flannel and blazer regalia.

Shatsie has changed from the pants suit in black gabardine she was wearing this afternoon to an identically tailored pants suit, in sado-masochist black silk. She has put a touch of red to her lips, and applied deep purple makeup into the sockets of her eyes so that she looks at the very least as interesting as any of the hookers seated on stools at the bar only a short distance away. She is smoking one of her cigars.

Although Diana is furnishing the tickets, Morrie has taken over the leadership of our group, and with perhaps a bit of extra unnecessary flamboyance, with one eye rarely straying from a somewhat bewildered looking Dr. Feigenweiser, he leads us up the staircase alongside the roped-in hordes of tourists waiting in line.

"That fuckin' Glick," Tony growls in my ear. "He prob'ly paid some asshole a couple hunnerd bucks to get us at the head of the line."

"And thank God, too," I say. Actually, I envy Morrie his ability to take charge in situations like this. He is a much better advance public relations man than I am, at least as far as handling social arrangements is concerned. I am pretty good with my press contacts, but when it comes to spending company money to pay off headwaiters, order gourmet dinners, and select expensive wines (usually entailing some embarrassing moments while he grills the wine steward), no one can touch Morrie.

We are, in fact, escorted to the head of the line, the roped-in multitudes eyeing us with hatred. We are ushered in two groups into a vast auditorium tiered in scallops of loge seats rising up from the festooned stage curtain at what seems like about a forty-degree incline. The Krauts are in a shell directly below us with Shatsie, who presumably will translate the words of Wayne Newton's songs to them. *"Jeder zeit es regnet, es regnet pfennigs von himmel."* Morrie has seen to it that Dr. Feigenweiser is with us in our pod.

Immediately Morrie is conferring with the waiter, a man who does not inspire confidence as a wine steward, but impresses rather as one of long experience in hard circumstances and somewhat in need of a shave. In his white jacket he looks like one of the hawkers who sell beer and hot dogs at Yankee stadium.

"Watch this," Tony rasps into my ear. "Don Perinyong, you wait."

Tony is wrong. The waiter reappears, accompanied by a second who could be his brother, each of them bearing standing ice buckets, glasses, and two bottles of Mumm's Cordon Rouge.

"Same price as the other," Tony says to me.

It is the conflict between man-on-the-road salesman versus what Tony perceives as the home office freeloader that so rankles and drives Tony to ruffle Morrie, if he can. To Morrie, he says, "What's the difference between Mumm's and Taylor's sparkling white, Glick?"

Morrie simply smiles at Tony condescendingly, and continues to focus his attention on Dr. Feigenweiser. "Do you like champagne, Doctor?"

Morrie is in his element now, and he watches every movement of the hot dog vendors to catch any dereliction of duty. Diana cannot keep her eyes off Morrie. It is his knowledge of the world and his dignified air of authority that have won her admiration and romantic favors.

Our waiter pours, strictly heeding Morrie's admonishment not to fill the glasses too high, then collects the company's gold American Express card which Morrie never leaves home without.

The bubbly is good, and we find ourselves looking at one another and grinning companionably as we take our first sips, just at the moment when the lights suddenly go down, the stage curtains are drawn up majestically, and a full orchestra rises from a pit in the middle of the stage, blasting forth with music so loud you can't make out the melody, and the darkness of the auditorium is splintered by a hundred vari-colored laser flashes streaking across the void from locations behind and to the sides of us. The effect is magnificent, irresistible, causing the skin to prickle, and each of us to stir about in our chairs as we experience a moment of magic and wonderment.

The audience, as a whole, leans perceptibly forward in anticipation of the star's entrance, as an offstage announcer, his voice rising above the blare of the music, a feat one would not have thought possible, booms out an introduction of:
"Mis-ter
　Way-y-y-y-y-ne
　　New-tu-u-u-u-u-u-u-u-u-nnnnnnn."
And out he comes, Mis-ter Way-y-y-y-y-ne New-tu-u-u-u-

u-u-u-u-u-u-nnnnn, in high-heeled snakeskin cowboy boots, purple velvet pants and a patterned shirt that looks like flocked wallpaper, loops of bracelets and bangles dangling and jangling from wrists and neck. His hair is greased back and looks like the black shiny stuff Morrie presumably puts on his shoes, and the little upswept black moustache can only be something pasted on at the last minute as some kind of joke aimed at henpecked husbands.

I immediately fear the worst, but having learned from experience that first impressions are not always right (though usually they are), settle back in my chair, applauding with the others, and wait for the show to proceed.

"Good evening, ladies and gentlemen," Wayne Newton chortles, as though this is the funniest gag of the evening (which I have the feeling it may very well be). The greeting is followed up by a couple of unfunny jokes about husbands not being with their wives, but the wives not being with their husbands, either. Which sends the audience into paroxyms of laughter, and me to a healthy quaff of my champagne. Morrie is grinning at the stage, and so is Diana. Dr. Feigenweiser looks like someone has just told him he has been cuckolded, and Tony is nudging Morrie and ostentatiously holding his nose.

We are then treated to a medley of 1940s swing band standards, designed to send chills up and down the spines of those in the audience over 50. Dr. Feigenweiser is looking very uncomfortable, and I notice that Tony now is chuckling and whispering in Morrie's ear. Morrie, stiffening, there is no doubt of it, keeps his eyes aimed at the stage, a determined grin frozen on his face.

"Ra-cing witha moo-oo-oo-oo-oo-oo-n

High abova silver—"

"You fucking son of a bitch!" Wayne's chorus is suddenly interrupted by Morrie screaming at Tony, at the same time leaping up abruptly from his chair, causing it to be knocked over, and toppling the champagne bucket, which, however, by moving quickly I am able to catch before it crashes to the floor.

"Whatsa matter?" Tony says, the facsimile of a grin on his face.

"*Vas is los?*" Dr. Feigenweiser is saying beside me.

"Cut it out, you guys!" I'm on my feet now, in between Morrie and Tony, facing Morrie. "Morrie! Cut it out!"

"Racing witha moo-oo-oo-oo-oo-n—"

"I'll kill the sonofabitch!" Morrie cries. And before the two Yankee stadium wine stewards who are rushing to our pod can get to us, Morrie has hauled back and thrown a haymaker which misses Tony but catches me on the left ear, hard enough so that more lasers go off, and instead of Wayne Newton, I hear a sudden loud ringing in the ears, which it occurs to me also could be the sound of Diana screaming at Tony, who ducks and steps back from her—all of this happening in an instant—and in doing so, suddenly tumbles backward over the balustrade of the loge into the arms of the waiting and grinning Krauts in the loge below, just as the wine stewards do finally reach us and roughly collar Morrie and me, one on each of us.

"Outside, you guys! Come on!" And there certainly is no arguing about it with them, as it turns out, I was right, they are basically not wine stewards, but bouncers. As we are bum rushed by some kind of jiujitsu hold around the neck, I catch a glimpse of Tony resting on his backside in the laps of the Krauts, grinning at us, and waving cheerily.

"You bastard!" Diana shouts at him, as Wayne Newton finally gives up, fearing perhaps that a riot is breaking out.

"Somebody's husband must have found somebody's wife!" he calls out. The audience roars with laughter, and Morrie and I are rushed up the steps, with Diana pulling at the bouncers and shouting at them that it isn't our fault, and Dr. Feigenweiser trying to keep up, puffing and wheezing and muttering, *"Nicht gut, nicht gut."*

Just before we reach the exit a hand reaches out of one of the topmost loges, and briefly I catch a glimpse in the dark of Loretta and Aldo Bellagamba, Loretta managing to touch me on the arm and saying, "Hey, lover, let's get together after for a nightcap!"

"All right, you guys, you feel better?" The bouncers have Morrie and me up against a wall, about three feet apart from each other now, one each holding us by the neck, looking more than ever as though they wouldn't mind throwing some kind of crippling punch now that we are out of sight of witnesses.

"We're not fighting," I say to the guy holding me.

"I'll say you're not."

"He was trying to separate them!" Diana puts in, to my everlasting gratitude.

"This guy?" says my bouncer. There is definitely a twinge of disapointment in his voice.

"Ja, iz all right now, chentlemens," says Dr. Feigenweiser.

"Who're you?" says my bouncer.

"A very highly placed scientist in our nation's defense effort," I manage to croak out at him. "Will you let go of my neck?"

The goon decides maybe he better let up. "No more funny stuff."

"Zere vill be no more vunny shtuvh," says Feigenweiser. "Zankyou, chentlemens."

Reluctantly, the bouncers withdraw back inside the auditorium, casting surly glances at us over their shoulders, and brushing their hands, as I would expect, in cliché fashion over their sleeves.

I look at Morrie. Suddenly he is crying. His head is in his hands, and his body is wracked with choking sobs.

"I'm sorry," he says. He looks at me with an of expression of such grief and misery that I feel momentarily like embracing him. But Diana takes care of it, slipping one arm around his waist now, and talking soothingly to him. "It's all right, Morrie. It's all right."

"Vut got into you, Mowwie?" Feigenweiser asks him.

"Nothing, it's nothing I can talk about," Morrie says.

"Iss tewwible image to pwoject of company," Feigenweiser says.

"Oh, fuck the company," Morrie says. And, it seems to me, it is his finest moment.

"Language, Morrie," Diana says.

"I'm sorry, Diana," Morrie says. And he really is. He looks at her with such sorrow and concern for her feelings that I am afraid he will burst into tears again.

"Don't worry about it, Morrie," I say.

"Ja," says Feigenweiser somewhat stiffly. "I zink I go to my womb now."

"It's been a long day," I find myself saying, and feeling foolish for doing so.

Feigenweiser clicks his heels, nods curtly, and departs to his womb, while Morrie, Diana and I stand awkwardly outside the arena, looking sheepishly at one another, as the crooning voice of Wayne Newton wafts thinly through the door.

"What happened, Morrie?" I ask him at last.

"That son of a bitch, Passanante," Morrie says, his face

contorting into rage again. "He's running a—a—raffle. He wanted me to ask Diana to volunteer as the prize."

"Oh, my God!"

"Oh, Morrie," Diana says, "so did you have to get all that excited?"

"You don't understand!" Morrie exclaims. "It—it—was—an insult!"

"We're all here to help out," Diana says soothingly. "What'd he want, me to go out on a dinner date, or something?"

"Eating was definitely a part of it," I toss in.

"Yeah," says Morrie bitterly. He looks at me sorrowfully. "Did I hit you, Brock?"

"Just sort of." My ear at the moment feels to be about as big as my head.

"Oh, Morrie, Morrie," Diana says. "Look at all the trouble, and just over a little jealousy."

"It wasn't jealousy!" Morrie shouts at her.

"Sh-sh-sh. Shush," she says, fingers to her lips. "You've got some explaining to do to Dr. Feigenweiser, too."

"Nazi prick," Morrie says.

"Language! Morrie!" She stomps her foot on the thick carpet.

She must be some wonderful piece in bed, because the price for anything less is more than anyone could possibly stand. There is no point in my hanging around any more. I figure the two of them will spend all night talking about it, without Diana ever having the slightest inkling of what Tony had proposed to Morrie, and, therefore, not the slightest inkling of what she is talking about, but she'll go on about it all night anyway, alternately consoling Morrie with a grind, then making him feel guilty by rolling her backside toward him.

"Good night, all," I say. I look at Morrie. The tuft of graying red hair that he grows on his left side is standing straight up in the air at the moment, giving him the wild look of a Samurai warrior in some old Japanese print. Actually, I can't help but feel that with it going straight up like that it gives him a look of dignity he ordinarily doesn't have.

"You did right, Morrie," I say to him. And even though I am just enough of a shit to find Tony Passanante's diabolical insult and assault on Diana's absurd notions of herself the most delicious part of the day, as a civilized human being I am obliged to add, "Tony's a prick, Morrie."

"Language!" Diana says.

CHAPTER V

The alarm goes off at 6:30, because I want to be up and at 'em and ready to skin 'em on the big day of the press conference. I assume it's another hot sunny day in Las Vegas, but it's impossible to tell from looking outside, since the hotel has rigged up some kind of exterior arrangement of blue neon lighting around all the windows that seeps into the room day and night simulating a perpetual twilight, a concession to gamblers, somebody told me, who don't want to be reminded that they have been up all night at their chores.

I bump into Morrie on the breakfast line, who tells me that Diana is catching a little extra sack time, information he has gathered, he says, by a phone call to her room.

"Poor kid," he says. "I guess she's all tuckered out."

Poor kid, probably from admiring herself all night in the ceiling mirror.

Morrie looks terrible, downtrodden and sad, but he makes no mention of the events of last evening. During breakfast he keeps glancing around the room nervously, hunching his shoulders and exhibiting a slight tic in his neck I have never noticed before. Finally, over coffee, he says, "Sorry about last night. Your ear looks terrible."

It feels terrible, but it will be all right. It is red and swollen, but I can hear all right, I don't have a headache, and the skin isn't broken. So I assume eventually it will recede back to something like normal.

Morrie and I share a cab together to the Convention Center, arriving at about eight, just as the first visitors to our concession already are beginning to drop in for free coffee at our air-conditioned refreshment bar. The air conditioning is a blessing, since the desert sun is hot as an oven, even at this early hour. Outside in the heat, Tony Passanante and his sales force are stationed at the various exhibit booths that line the main mall.

In the executive offices, I find Dr. Feigenweiser conferring with Shatsie, who is on the phone to Germany where it is two o'clock in the afternoon. Dr. Feigenweiser is cordial, but hardly genial. I show him the press kits with his treatise included, and he is pleased. The plan is for the press to arrive at about noon. After Diana checks them in at a reception desk, they will take chairs at the café tables in the piazza, and I will greet them from a podium next to a long table behind which will be seated Dr. Feigenweiser, Frank, Morrie and Tony. Dr. Feigenweiser and I, without going into the events of last night, agree that Tony and Morrie should be seated at opposite ends of the table.

"Vill Mowwie go gwazy again?" Dr. Feigenweiser asks.

"No," I say. "He was provoked."

My part of the day's activities is all set, with very little for me to do from now until noon, when the press is scheduled to arrive. I had intended simply to distribute the press kits, then ask Morrie to give a brief demonstration of the Hand-Arbiter, using a prop, take a few questions, then call a halt to the business part of the meeting, and invite everyone to sit down and enjoy a "picnic lunch box" of paté, cold shrimps, a pimento and avocado salad, and a pastry for dessert. White wine (which, diplomatically, I deferred to Morrie to select—a modest Sancerre), and, finally, a cup of coffee, will send them on their way with a warm glow and a press kit full of information about Hand-Arbiter to copy from back at their offices and print verbatim in the next month's issuance of their magazines. Dr. Feigenweiser's interjection, of course, will alter this schedule, with him making the major presentation, for twenty-five minutes, after which the Foreign Legionnaires will shake rubber hands all around, and then offer their palms for close inspection and fondling by the press, a bit of business that I have the feeling may turn everybody off from portions of the cold pimento and avocado salad. Anyway, that's a few hours away.

Now, at 8:30, three aides, or usherettes, show up, and are briefed by Shatsie in her office. These are local Vegas girls whom we rent from an agency to stand around in hot pants with farmer-in-the dell suspenders over tee shirts and wearing straw hats. On the front of the tee shirts, in and out of the valleys, you can make out the company's name, PRO-TEC. Since one of the major objects of an exposition of this kind is to attract sales leads, the girls have as their assignment to direct any visitors to our area toward a table with a giant glass bowl on it into which they are invited to drop their name, address, affiliation, and an indication of whether or not they want to receive sales literature and a sales call follow-up. (They'll get the sales literature whether they say they want it or not.) Every day at the hour of noon, one of the girls will draw a slip from the glass bowl, and read the name of a winner over the public address system, winners being entitled to a two-week vacation for two to Hawaii, or a free prosthetic device of their choice. These prosthetic devices are not cheap, so anyone with a leg missing, or whatever, might very well choose the plastic replacement, at least such is the thinking of our leader, Frank, whose brainchild this lottery drawing is. Of course, there are a lot of distributors and dealers here at the exposition, and if a guy has already been to Hawaii and doesn't want to go again, even if his own limbs are all intact, he might choose the prosthetic device which he could then sell through his outlet back home and use the money from the sale for a trip to Paris for two weeks. So maybe Frank knows what he's doing, at that. At first, Frank just wanted to offer the prosthetic device, but Tony, I think it was, persuaded him to offer the trip to Hawaii as an alternative, in case the winner didn't want the inconvenience of carrying a plastic leg home with him on the plane. Actually, this drawing is rather generous, at least in comparison with what other exhibitors are offering, things like free fountain pens and pocket calculators. The Krauts have arranged for the Pro-Tec barrage balloon overhead to circle around trailing a banner reading: "BIG PRIZES AT PRO-TEC." This, it is anticipated, will stimulate traffic to our exhibit area.

It looks as though everything is under control; the food is scheduled to arrive from a concessionaire at 11:45, with a crew of waitresses in white uniforms to serve it.

I step outside, and except for my throbbing ear, feel fairly comfortable with myself. The sky is deep blue, the sun high, and I raise my face to catch a few minutes of the last rays of summer and perhaps darken my complexion just slightly so that when I return home to Connecticut everyone who sees me will think I am a playboy who vacations all summer, or at the least, a world traveler moving through romantic places. As I look upward, the barrage balloon floats before my eyes, with its trailer: "BIG PRICES AT PRO-TEC." A nice promotional touch. We have completely dominated the competition at this exposition. Big *PRICES!* What the hell is going on?! *PRIZES,* for Christ sake!

I scurry into the executive suite and interrupt Shatsie dialing Germany again.

"Shatsie! Shatsie! Hold the phone!" I bawl at her. She hangs up.

"Who ordered the sign on the barrage balloon?"

"I did," she says, a look of pride crowding aside her normally depraved expression.

"It says, 'Big prices.'"

"Ja," she says. "Zat's vot I told zem—big pwi-ces."

"Prizes! Shatsie! Prizes!"

"Oh! Mit an 's'."

"Mit a 'z'!"

"Mit a 'z'," Shatsie says. "So ve spell it wight now." And she goes for the phone again.

For the rest of the morning, traffic at the Pro-Tec exhibit is heavy. Tony and his men are busy waving plastic arms and hearts at holiday-spirited groups of distributors and dealers who have come to our area to check out the latest developments in prosthetics while helping themselves to free coffee and Danish pastries and enjoying the air-conditioned comfort of our sultan's tent. Our farmerette hostesses don't let them escape without getting their entries into the daily raffle.

At 11:30, Frank arrives in a taxi, accompanied by Diana. (She sure manages to be in the right place always at the right time.) When Frank walks down the center mall of the exhibit area, it's a little like a general inspecting the troops. Everyone stands just a little straighter, except the Vegas farmerette hostesses who try to interest him in taking a chance on a trip to Hawaii.

I encounter him at the entrance to the circus tent, as I have just finished setting up the speaker's table and tested the microphone.

"Good morning, Frank."

"Wha hoppen to y'ear?" he says.

"Oh? Oh, my ear? Oh, ho. That's a story."

"You guys do too much drinkin'. We're not out here ta play. We're here ta do a job."

"Everything's all set, Frank."

"It better be." And he moves on inside.

"He's cute," Diana says to me. And then adds, "How's Morrie?"

"He's fine. For a guy that didn't sleep much last night."

"What do you mean, didn't sleep much?" She glares at me, the crease between her eyes deepening for a moment, looking as though it will cleave her head.

"Restless, you know."

"Oh."

The food arrives, as scheduled, at 11:45. My press guys, loyal bunch that they are, and hungry, start arriving just before noon. We have plenty of food. There is a slight delay of the press conference while we wait for one of the farmerettes to pull the name of today's winner of the trip to Hawaii.

"Mr. and Mrs. Aldo Bellagamba!" she calls out.

I am not even surprised. A little hurt, perhaps, that Aldo and Loretta didn't bother to look me up and say hello.

The press people have been touring the convention area since nine o'clock, and already their briefcases are full of press releases which they have picked up. They have the whole afternoon and evening and two more days of this, so they are glad enough to be seated and ready for lunch. Scattered amongst them as inconspicuously as possible are the ten Krauts in navy blazers and gray flannels who will rise at the end of Dr. Feigenweiser's presentation, and shake hands with the journalist of their choice, and then offer a close-up individualized working demonstration of how the Hand-Arbiter works.

I know these press people, and am comfortable and informal with them. Even the guys I don't know I greet familiarly, so that Frank, who is watching me closely, probably to discern any signs of lapsing dignity, will get the impression that my press contacts are indispensable to the company's success.

"Hey, Joe! Good to see you, buddy!" Reading the name "Joseph Meechum" on the lapel of one fellow I have never before seen in my life.

"Is this the Sport Supporter press luncheon?" Mr. Meechum asks in a loud voice. Sport Supporter, our major competitor.

"Sh-h-h-h-h! Not so loud. Yes, it is, Joe. Sit right down. You'll have the opportunity in a few minutes of meeting the president of our company!"

I tell Diana to get the guy aside, and run his ass the hell off the premises.

"Language!" she says.

With everyone seated, I greet the press corps in a casual kind of way, but with a dignified presentation, sort of the way a professional toastmaster might do it, not neglecting to underline the main point that in the press kits laid out on the tables at their various places they will be able to read about a prosthetic device that is "light years ahead of anything the industry has yet devised."

"And here to describe the background connected with the development of Pro-Tec's new Hand-Arbiter prosthetic device is the inventor himself, Dr. Wolfgang Feigenweiser!"

It is incredible to me to hear Dr. Feigenweiser speaking now, in his German accent, which somehow seems twice as impermeable as in normal conversation. With medical references to metatarsals and femurs and occipital regions, the press guys after the first five minutes are growing restive. Larry Hopkins, Editor-in-Chief, of *The American Review,* who is generally acknowledged as the dean of the prosthetic device journalists, sets what I suddenly have a premonition may turn out to be an unfortunate example by rising from his seat at about eight minutes into Feigenweiser's dissertation and slipping over to me.

"Good meeting," he says out of the side of his mouth. "I got all your stuff." He pats the kit of press material. "I'll do a nice job for you in the next issue."

"Gee, thanks, Larry. Aren't you going to stay for lunch?"

"I'd like to, really. But the Sport Supporter guys are having an affair in five minutes. I promised I'd show up."

"Oh, well. Sure. I understand. Thanks for coming by, Larry."

I am still shaking his hand goodbye, when Fred Payntor, Managing Editor of *Precision Prosthetics,* comes at me from the other side.

"Good meeting," he says out of the side of his mouth. "I got all your stuff." He pats the kit of press material. "I'll do a nice job for you in the next issue."

"Gee, thanks, Fred. Aren't you going to stay for lunch?"

"I'd like to, really. But the Sport Supporter guys are having an affair in five minutes. I promised I'd show up."

"Oh, well. Sure. I understand. Thanks for coming by, Fred."

Two guys are standing next to me, the editor and the publisher of *Prosthetic Technology,* with the same story as the others.

Feigenweiser has fifteen minutes more to go, and the editors of my three top magazines of the industry have walked out. Surveying the room, I can see others in the audience, looking about them, vying to see who will be the next to rise and come over without appearing too unseemly about it.

Joe Meechum, the guy whom I did not know when I greeted him familiarly a few minutes before, is the next to approach me.

"Good meeting," he says out of the side of his mouth. "I got all your stuff." He pats the kit of press material. "I'll do a nice job for you in the next issue."

"Gee, thanks, Joe. Aren't you going to stay for lunch?"

"I'd like to, really. But the Pro-Tec guys are having an affair in five minutes. I promised I'd show up."

I've got to get Feigenweiser to cut his speech short before they all leave. I slip away from another reporter whom I see coming at me with regrets, and make my way up to the head table. I tiptoe around behind the Pro-Tec management people, trying to demonstrate that if I am not invisible, at least I am respectful. Out in the audience, two more journalists have moved to the back, and are waving at me, as they leave. I wave back, as Frank revolves his head on his neck in my direction, and glares at me. I sit down in an empty chair near Feigenweiser, and give him a little tap on the shoulder, as he drones on. But either he is so deep in concentration over his text that he is oblivious to all else, or his shoulder is made of some kind of artificial material that doesn't respond to the touch. He does not pause.

"Ss-s-s-s-s-s-t-t-t-t-t, Dr. Feigenweiser," I hiss at him.

"Quiet!" I hear behind me. It is Frank, looking as though he is about to get up from his seat and give me a dignified belt in the mouth.

There is nothing to do. Feigenweiser drones on. My press guys keep slinking out the back, looking up at the last minute, and making little A-OK signs with thumb and forefinger, or waving good-bye. One guy tosses me a kiss. Not so with Mary Deegan, Managing Editor of *Arms, Legs, Etc.* She waits to catch my eye, then rolls her eyes heavenward, as if commiserating with me, and turns and flees.

I sit with the others, as Feigenweiser, after close to twenty-five minutes, finally grinds to the end of his paper. "I zink zat gifs evwybody a pwetty gut picture of Hand-Arbeiter," he says, reaching for a glass of water, "zo I vill now ask now my associates in ze audience to wise und ingwoduce zemselves to you, und you can ask zem anyzing you vish."

At that point, the entire audience that remains seated in front of us rises, there being no journalists left among them, only the ten Krauts, who after a moment of looking consternated, turn to each other, and shake hands genially.

"I hope you will all stay for lunch," I say quickly, and slink away from the table to the men's room, both to be alone for a moment to think, and to wait until the nausea passes.

There is nothing to think about, except that probably I will be blamed for not tying the journalists to the tables, and the nausea does pass, so I go out to face the music.

"How did zey like my pwesentation?" Dr. Feigenweiser asks, intercepting me quickly.

"Not bad, Doctor. Not bad. I think we'll get good press coverage." Which is the truth. Though I will never have credibility with any of my contacts again.

"Gut," he says, adding, "Frank is looking for you."

I don't want to see Frank, but, of course, there is no avoiding him. He is seated at a table with a plate already in front of him, chewing on a shrimp, and brandishing a glass of Diet Pepsi in one hand."

"Wha' hoppened?" he growls at me.

"Everybody had all the material they needed. We'll get good press coverage, Frank."

"Wha'd dey all walk out fa?"

Guess, you asshole! I almost say it, but thinking of my family, my company pension investiture (due not until another six months) I manage instead to smile thinly.

"Sport Supporter was holding a press conference simulta-neously, Frank. The guys came to ours first as a courtesy to me, then felt they had to go over there."

"Oh? Okay. Siddown and eat."

And that's the end of it. My part of the conference is over. I can catch a jet out that afternoon, comfortable in the knowl-edge that Feigenweiser will go back to Germany and tell everyone that they loved his presentation in Vegas; Frank is reasonably satisfied that we have held a successful press con-ference; Pro-Tec will get the publicity that the journalists promised; Tony will get his blow job; Morrie will have had two nights with Diana; and I go home with a cauliflower ear to see my dear wife and find out if there is news of how my son is doing at his prep school. These thoughts all occur as my mind races forward to the next step in my life, which will occur in my 51st year, because today, I suddenly remember, is my 50th birthday.

CHAPTER VI

I'm able to catch an evening 6:45 plane out of Vegas, which means that I'll get into LaGuardia at 12:30 midnight, Eastern time, just barely in time to catch the last limo to Connecticut, assuming we're not late, in which case, if we are, to hell with it, I'll splurge and take a taxi.

The convention will be going on for two more days, with a cocktail reception scheduled for tonight by the pool at Caesar's Palace, which Tony and his sales group are putting on for about 150 Pro-Tec customers. They don't need me any more, as the press is not invited. There will be a band, plus what I will describe in next month's *Pro-Tec News* as a "sumptuous buffet," and twenty minutes of one-liners by a Vegas comic who has been warned not to make sick jokes about paraplegics this time, as a certain lapse in taste two years ago cost Pro-Tec one of its biggest accounts.

"Welcome aboard Flight 567, ladies and gentlemen. I'm Captain Dowd—" Get outta here! Well, at least, if I need it, I've got a ride up to Connecticut from the airport in a Jeep Wagoneer.

We have a light load, and those aboard are subdued, having perhaps all thrown away their life savings at the gambling tables. The two seats next to me are empty, and once we are in

71

the air I am able to sprawl out and slump down reasonably comfortably with a blanket and pillow. It is unlikely that I will be able to sleep, but lulled by the hypnotic thrum of the jet engines, and with the pressure of the cabin increasingly blocking my ears, I will turn within myself, as is my habitude on night flights such as these, and muse for a couple of hours.

As always, in such circumstances, what surfaces in my mind is the question, What am I doing with my life? Whether this kind of self-questioning is common to all business travelers, or unique to me, I am not sure. In any event, today particularly (on my 50th birthday), I cannot help but wonder, cannot escape the question. At precisely half a hundred years, statistically two-thirds of my life is behind me, gone. Maybe I have twenty-five years remaining. Of those, probably fifteen are left with any energy in them. I will die, and I will have accomplished: what?

Of course, the relevant question is what would I like to have accomplished? And, in truth, I am not really sure that I know, not sure really if there is anything I might have done, or even could do yet, that might fulfill the hopeful notions that I once had about my life. Whatever they were. I don't know that they were ever that specific.

They were most intense, I suppose, in Paris, and would have had to do with being a poet, and doing exciting things. With emphasis, I think, largely on the doing of exciting things. Which is no more specific than what I can come up with now. Maybe I would have said travel. Hey, well, here I am, traveling.

Of course, this trip is not quite up to what I would have had in mind then, that being something more along the lines of, say, a trip to Sweden to accept the Nobel prize for poetry, with the world's press crowding in on me at the reception and asking my opinion on important subjects such as human rights and perestroika.

Poetry is out. The only writing I do now is for Pro-Tec at the office, and once a month putting my signature on a batch of checks at my cluttered desk in my tiny den/office off the living room at home. Now and then I write a letter to my father, and once a year or so I get a letter off to the editor of the weekly *Courier* about something or other of importance, like the menace of dog-doo on the town sidewalks.

It is true, I do spend a lot of time in that little office. Sometimes at the cluttered desk, but more often in my Air-Flow recliner, chewing on a Bic or reading *The New Yorker*, or the *Courier*, or sometimes nodding off to sleep.

That is not the way I envisioned it would be when I was twenty-four and living in Paris.

Life was to be a perpetual Nobel Prize ceremony, and what it turns out to be is getting up at 6:30 A.M. five days a week (except when I take trips to Las Vegas and other places and get up at 4:30), driving to work in fairly heavy traffic, spending the day being cheerful and fending off requests to do things that I do not want to do for the likes of Diana, Tony, Morrie, Frank and a half dozen others. And arriving home at 6:30 at night, sitting with drink in hand in our country kitchen/family room while my wife steps around me and puts on dinner.

Generally, we finish dinner at eight. I watch one or two television situation comedies, waiting for the pre-meal cocktail and dinner wine to dissipate, and then drag myself into my den/office and instead of writing a poem, I stare at a report that Frank has been waiting to see for two weeks.

On weekends, I play tennis doubles on Saturday morning with a bunch of guys out here whom I don't see except on the tennis court. Saturday afternoons, the kids and I take the garbage to the dump, then deposit bottles at the supermarket, and maybe there's an hour or two left during which my wife and I go to local nurseries (in summer) and look at plants and come back and put them in the ground, or we go to the hardware store (in winter) and buy washers and nuts and bolts and screws and nails, and bang at this or that door, latch, cover, window frame, porch step, curtain rod, or whatever. Saturday nights my wife and I go out to dinner and to a movie, or once in a while to somebody's house for a party, say, like Chet Dowd's, which usually depresses me beyond bearance.

Sundays we read the *Times,* and try to avoid going to "brunches," and catch up on yard work, and do something with the kids (who increasingly now don't want to do anything with us, because they have things of their own to do), then watch "60 Minutes" in the evening before retiring back into my den/office to psyche up to get ready for another week at Pro-Tec.

This is not living. And yet, it is what I do. Week after week, month after month, year after year. Along the way we have a few laughs (not too many) and some fights (not too many, and noted previously). But there is missing that notion held once in Paris that life some day would be a continuing and an intense involvement with literary success and fame.

But this is useless woolgathering. Even if I had been any good as a poet and had stayed with it, I wonder if I wouldn't be feeling the same sense of missed opportunities and regret that I feel now. The only one of our poetry group in Paris who actually did go on to pursue the literary life, Pritch Bates,

74

managed to squeeze out a half-dozen largely ignored lifeless novels in which with increasing bitterness he blamed his mother, his father, his sister, his ex-wives and whatever former friends he once had for the miserable mess he has since made of his life. His most recent novel, *A Loser, Whining,* was dismissed by a reviewer for the Sunday *Times Book Review* with the cryptic summary: "Put it back in the sand, Pritch."

Hemingway said somewhere, before he blew his head off, that the hardest thing in his life was getting through from one day to the next—after the day's work was done.

I can understand that. Work, at least, while it was good, and made sense, gave Hemingway courage to live. Then the work got boring for him. And that was it.

What gives me courage? I don't know. Certainly not my work. Fear, maybe. I live in terror, really, of being canned, though I make a manful effort to whatever extent I can not to think about it. What I do is I struggle mightily day after day to make myself indispensable to the company so that when they go through one of their periodic cost cutbacks and result-ant "house-cleanings," I won't be swept out with the others. That's all. I don't feel any sense of "loyalty" to Pro-Tec. Any more than Pro-Tec's powers-that-be feel any "loyalty" to me. If I weren't selling plastic hand jobs for Pro-Tec, the first place I'd go looking to make a living for my family would be to Pro-Tec's number one competitor, Sport Supporter. During the past ten years I've managed to survive three housecleanings, and each time it gets more terrifying, simply because the longer I am there, the larger my salary gets, and I live in fear that Mac McDougall, the Vice President of Finance, one of these days will get the bright idea that somebody else younger than I could do my job just as well (better?) than I can at half the salary. And he's probably right! Sure, it would take them a year to break the guy in to the level of proficiency that I have, but they could do it. And I have no written contract with the company. Presumably they might give me three months' severance pay, but three months isn't all that long to find a job on my level, and at my age. Even supposing somebody would want me. Who would want me? Sport Supporter? If I asked for the same salary I'm getting at Pro-Tec, they would pass. If I asked for less, they might wonder what the hell was wrong with me.

What if I had to move to another city? I mean, to someplace like Houston? I've got nothing against Houston, but I couldn't live there. It's just not me. It would be like taking a Macintosh apple tree and planting it in Texas. It would die. They have their own apples, and they're probably pretty good, but they're not Macintosh.

Naturally, I try to cover up my fears in the presence of other people. I suspect that Morrie and Tony think I'm one of the easiest-going guys they know, and Frank, as noted earlier, has a persistent suspicion that I am a wise guy and a con man. Which I am not! I was trying to be loose with the guy! To put him at ease by my own easiness with him. And because he has no sure confidence in himself, he mistook my easy *style* as some kind of lapse in dignity.

He doesn't know what dignity is. Dignity isn't wearing a navy blazer with Mickey Mouse brass buttons and gray flannels, and having a staff of 100 salesmen let little farts in their pants when you tour the premises.

Morrie thinks dignity lies in being called Morris, instead of Morrie, and wearing his hair in a sheaf tossed over his bald spot and showing off in front of the Krauts by scolding waiters about the wine. When he said, "Fuck the company" to Feigen-weiser, that was dignity. And Morrie doesn't even realize it. He'll hate himself for having said it for the rest of his life, and if he tries to forget about it, Diana won't let him; she will pester him for having lost his "composure" because he happened to have had enough dignity to resent Tony's suggestion that she should give head for a hundred dollar bill.

Dignity, for Christ sake. Dignity is not sitting calmly in your chair looking like the RCA Victor pooch while the Krauts, or anybody else, spout insane ideas that should be shot down and shouted down for what they are, a lot of megalomaniacal self-serving shit! Sitting there and saying nothing may be an exercise in self-control, I'll grant that. And no doubt, too, self-control is a virtue in life. But it is not really dignity.

I may not know what it is, dignity. And maybe it is something that forever will elude me. But I know what it is *not*. And I know, further, that whatever it is, or however one finds a way of living with it, it must have something to do with kindness, or compassion, or gentleness, or something very close to those three things. Which, to my mind, are not merely words to be mouthed in order to dupe others into accepting whatever deceptions at the moment serve one's self-interested purposes.

I think that very likely I am not attuned to the world. Probably I am a misfit, though I am able to hide it from most people. A neurotic. Certainly I am confused. Bemused, too. And bewildered. My powers laid waste, I feel. Late and soon, getting and spending, my heart given away. How do those lines go? "—Great God! I'd rather be

A Pagan suckled in a creed outworn;

77

So might I, standing on this pleasant lea,"
(Half sleeping while Chet flies the plane)
"Have glimpses that would make me less forlorn;
Have sight of Proteus rising from the sea;
Or hear old Triton blow his wreathed horn."

Jesus! Who wouldn't have wanted to be a poet after reading that for the first time?

My son, whom I have not thought of in two days, is entering into this world that I find myself overwhelmed by. Without ever having read Wordsworth or even *The New York Times,* he recognizes that we are preparing him for a bucket of shit. Is it any wonder that he wants no part of anything that he associates with his old man, which in his mind is indistiguishable from adult life? He sees himself as an outlaw, and nourishes the fantasy. An outlaw in the sense that he is outside the constraints of the rest of us, even though it is not in his nature, I don't think, to break any actual laws. It is the notion of himself as outside, the hobo around the campfire, that he cherishes right now. And who is to say that he is wrong? And yet, what are we doing, my wife and I? We hope that if that $11,000-a-year school that we are sending him to does its job right, within four years he will be elbowing others out of the way to get into Harvard Business School and come out and get his own job in marketing and join the parade. Believe me, if he wants to be a poet, and shows the slightest talent at it, he'll get no argument from me. I'll help him. I'm not trying to force him into anything. Give him his shot in life. Maybe I will write this down, and give it to him. It will help us to understand each other better. He is, in a sense, the only monument that I will ever create, and all I ask is that it turn out *right.*

CHAPTER VII

Chet puts us down smoothly and on time into LAG, and I get lucky with the Connecticut limo, having to wait around the baggage area for only ten minutes before they call out my name.

At the Norwalk stop, I retrieve the Pontiac from the darkened parking lot, hubcaps still in place, and twenty-five minutes later, at exactly 2:45 A.M. on the dashboard digital clock/radio, I am turning into the driveway of the old homestead. (Ahead of Chet apparently, as his Wagoneer is not in the driveway where he customarily parks it when he's there).

My wife has left the front porch light on for me, which is a welcoming sight to a weary breadwinner. I let myself in quietly so as not to wake her, wrestle the bags into the hall, and pass on through to the country kitchen/family area where I am somewhat taken aback to find her sitting in her pajamas and robe at the kitchen table, reading *The New York Times*.

"Hi," she says.

After eighteen years of marriage, a sense of a break in the normal household rhythm signals that something is wrong. "How come you're up?"

She looks up at me from the newspaper without speaking,

her gaunt expression seemingly mirroring the day's headlined tragedies.

"What's wrong?"

And in the next moment her face is buried in her hands, her shoulders heaving, and little helpless squeaking noises are coming from deep within her.

"What happened?!"

"Peter—"

I reach out for support from the back of a chair.

"He's been—suspended!"

Suspended! I thank God it's only that. In a daze, I say, "Suspended."

"For smoking—pot."

And, incredibly, I am aware of the sick hollow terror of the preceding moment already becoming transformed into a new feeling, of fury at my son. "When?"

"Last night. Mr. Lacy called. I didn't want to call you in Vegas."

"How long's he suspended for?"

"Until Christmas!" It comes out as a choked cry.

"Christmas!"

My wife nods her head wordlessly. She is crying softly now, and I realize that probably she has been crying most of the day. Her face is red from long hours of her grief, and wet, as she brushes the sleeve of her gown across her eyelids.

She is crying for the same reason that I feel like screaming. We have sent our son away to this school to save his life, and within three days of being there he has decided to end it. For that is what it means, it seems to me. They are to send him back from the sanctuary, back into the plague.

Possibly there are mitigating circumstances. "Were there other kids involved?"

"Just one."

"A bad kid?"

"Mr. Lacy says Peter was the instigator."

"I can't stand it!"

"That's why they want to send him home. They say—they think he's a bad influence."

A bad influence. You have to hear this said—that your kid is a bad influence—to really know what it is to have failed in life. I may not have become a Nobel prize laureate poet; the daily routine at Pro-Tec I may find absurd and ultimately demeaning; but all of that I can absorb and accept; I would cheerfully—gratefully—put up with the worst imaginable humiliations for the rest of my life—until the very moment they lower me into the ground—if the monument that my wife and I have labored over for fifteen years, our son, might turn out to be a thing of pride and beauty. To hear that this only creation is *unacceptable*—rejected—is to know absolute and total failure.

"We've got to do something."

"Mr. Lacy will be in his office tomorrow at nine. He says you can call him then."

"When does he want Peter out?"

"Today. He wanted him out today. I told him you were away. So he said tomorrow."

"Have they got him behind bars?" As wrong as my son is, I can't help feeling a first tinge of resentment that the school is acting so swiftly and vengefully. By kicking him out—for that's what they might as well be doing if they suspend him until Christmas—they are throwing him back into the same den of wolves that we had hoped to rescue him from. He will be lost. I understand well that the school must have its rules and must make an example, but at what cost to the poor little bastard who got nailed? He's not an addict, for Christ sake! He's a jerk! A show-off little kid whom they should scare the hell out of by sending him home for a week, if they have to, then bring back on probation with a warning that one tiny slip again, and it's out not until Christmas, but until 2010 A.D. The kid—any kid—deserves that chance, to see if he can learn anything from a dumb mistake and turn himself around 180 degrees, and win all the senior awards on commencement day three years from now. That's what I have to tell Lacy on the phone tomorrow.

And I will convince him that I am right! Not for nothing have I spent the past ten years of my life bullshitting editors to run terrible half-truths and lies about Pro-Tec products in their magazines and doing it successfully enough so that I have a solid reputation in the field, and have survived corporate housecleanings and have gotten raises, and, with the exception of Frank, have most people fooled into thinking I have a certain amount of dignity. My son must be allowed to continue.

But for the moment, at three o'clock in the morning, there is nothing more that my wife and I can say to one another about what has happened. We are both exhausted.

Before retiring upstairs, my wife takes time to go into the other room, returning a moment later with a little box wrapped in gay birthday wrapping paper. "It's a hell of a birthday," she says, "but I hope your 51st year is a happy one."

"Thanks," I say. It's a hell of a time to have to give me a

birthday present. I take it from her, and open it, feigning eagerness, as if nothing has happened.

Inside the box is an electronic radar detecting device—a fuzz buster—that I have been threatening to buy for myself ever since I got my last speeding ticket. I look up at my wife, genuinely pleased.

"You wanted one," she says. "I knew you wouldn't spend the money on yourself."

"It's a good one, too," I say. I love it. It can be attached under the grill, and the control will fit for concealment in the ashtray. I give my wife a small kiss on the lips. "Thanks, hon. It's a nice present."

"I'm sorry this is such a terrible day for your birthday," she says.

"It doesn't matter. What is important is that we get through this."

She gives me a small wan smile, and turns to go upstairs. I make the rounds of the downstairs rooms, turning out lights.

Once in our double bed, my wife mercifully, I can tell from her regular and heavy breathing, falls off to sleep, almost immediately. Having passed on to me the burden of the day's unhappy developments, she is able, at last, to slip away now, while I remain there beside her, rigid, tense, and in my wide-awake state, fending off one by one the unceasing procession of demons of this longest of all nights.

How much sleep comes to me I do not know, but at seven o'clock, I am vaguely aware of coming out of a semi-conscious state. It was after four when I last looked at the clock. So I have logged perhaps three hours. Which will be enough to get me out of bed, and freshened up, and to the phone to talk to Mr. Lacy and plead for my son's life.

Coffee is all that I can keep down for breakfast. I am literally sick, as is my wife. The two of us circle each other, and cross paths, and sigh, and shake our heads, and wait for the minutes to tick by so that I can call Lacy at nine o'clock.

Actually, I put in the call at 8:55, and his secretary answers.

"May I tell him who is calling please?"

"William Brock. Peter's father?"

"Oh, *yes,* Mr. Brock." As if she knows all about it, along with the whole of the rest of the school, and can't wait to put me through to find out how all of this will turn out.

"Hel-lo." Lacy sort of sings it out. I have the feeling he has had the best night's sleep of his life, and is freshly shaved and cologned and ready to knock over the day's ducks as they stick up their heads.

"Mr. Lacy. William Brock here." I have this affected silly notion picked up from some old Richard Burton movie, I suppose, that this is a more impressive way of announcing myself than just saying, "This is Bill Brock." Letting the guy on the other end know that this is no ordinary jerk here, that I went to Amherst, or Yale, or Princeton, or some such.

"Who?"

The little bastard, he knows who. His secretary just told him. "Bill Brock, Peter's father."

"Hold on, please." The phone clicks off in my ear.

What's going on? Is he punishing me? *I* didn't get caught smoking dope.

"Yes, hello," he says at last, coming back on. Incredibly, I get the impression he has had me on hold while going to the fruit bowl, because it sounds now like he's eating a peach, or something.

"I'm calling about Peter," I say.

"Yes." Slurp. "Are you coming up to fetch him?"

"I was wondering if we could talk a minute about his suspension."

"Yes. Until Christmas vacation. I spoke to the boy's mother."

"My wife."

"Yes."

"I would like to put in, if I may, Mr. Lacy, a word on Peter's behalf." I'm working very hard at trying to be deferent without actually sounding obsequious.

"Yes?" Which I take to be a probationary permission to continue.

"I wonder if you have had a chance to talk to Peter at all." (I know fucking well he hasn't; too busy, out sucking around alumni and parents for endowments for the school. Christ! I'll contribute! If he'll play ball with me—I'll donate—I swear, he can have the house!)

"He is not a bad boy, Mr. Lacy. Certainly he is no drug addict. He is not incorrigible. He is a good boy who has made a serious mistake. I believe right now—more than ever before in his life—he needs to be at your school. I know this boy's heart. I believe that if you will let him be in your school, his gratitude ultimately will express itself in the form of his leadership abilities, of which he has many. I would like to ask you to reconsider, if it is at all possible, the term of his suspension. I would like to ask you talk to him; tell him how close he has come to cutting off his life; how he can save himself now by turning himself around. I believe that will do him more good than a three-month suspension. I know that you have the rest of the school to think of. I hope you do not really believe that he will corrupt the others. I know that an example must be set. But, please—I would like to ask you to consider sending him home for a shorter period. Set a necessary example, certainly. But with compassion, possibly save an unformed youngster from being lost. I'm asking you to consider giving him that chance, if you can, sir."

There is silence on the other end of the line, except for something that sounds like the licking of fingers.

"I haven't talked with his advisor yet," he says, finally.

"Would it be helpful to do that, sir?"

"He's scheduled to come in."

"Could you make a final decision after that, then?"

There is another pause. "I'll get back to you."

"I'll be here, sir. I'll be ready to come up and fetch him on a minute's notice."

"Within the hour," he says, and hangs up.

I am left with a buzzing phone in my hand, as though having been dismissed, as customarily, by Frank. I am paying this guy $11,000 a year, and he's dumping on me as though I were trying to sell him life insurance. But, of course, that's the point; I am.

I put the device into the cradle, and moving quickly now past the anxious eyes of my wife who follows my lurching progress into the downstairs bathroom, I manage to get down to my knees in time in front of the bowl and heave my empty insides into the circle of water.

"Oh, Bill," my wife says, behind me in the doorway, not knowing what to do.

"'Sokay," I say, and reach for a handful of toilet paper from the roll that has been replaced since missing three days ago, and wipe the rancid slime off my lips. "There's nothing more we can do."

86

We have the hour to wait. It's already 9:15, and I am already long overdue at the office. I call now to tell Jinny, my secretary, (whom I share with Tony Passanante) that I doubt if I'll be in today.

"Too much Las Vegas, I guess," is what I say, an inane excuse calculated to appeal to what I tend to think is expected of me. "Little tummy upset." Under the circumstances, not exactly an untruth.

"Dieter Grunsted called from overseas," she reports. "He needs a publicity shot of the Vegas display."

"Call him back. You can still catch him before they close for the day. Tell him a set of both color prints and black and white prints is being sent by Express Mail directly from the photographer in Vegas. He should have them early next week."

"Also, a reporter, Joe Meechum. Says he met you yesterday at the Sport Supporter press conference, and wants to talk to you about Hand-Arbiter."

"I met him at the Pro-Tec conference!"

"That's what I thought."

"Anybody else?"

"Not yet."

"If Tony or Morrie calls from Vegas, tell them I'm out seeing editors. I'll call you back later in the day."

"Okay."

"Thanks, Jinny. Next time Tony is out of the office, you got a day off, on me."

"I'll buy that."

I can't afford to ignore Joe Meechum. If he can figure out where he was yesterday, he could do me some good. He must be on valium or something. In any event, I'm grateful to have some business to occupy my attention until Lacy calls back.

I call Meechum on the children's phone, so as to keep the line open to Lacy. My wife promises to hang up on anybody else who calls on our phone.

"Joe! Bill Brock here. How are ya?! . . . You got back okay? . . . Last night? . . . . Me, too . . . What can I do for ya? . . . Hey, Joe, that was the *Pro-Tec* display I met you at yesterday . . . Right! We make Hand-Arbiter. Sport Supporter makes a piece of shit called E-Z Clamp. It's no good. A guy put one on—This is no bullshit, Joe—he put one on, and grabbed his pecker to take a leak, and the goddamn thing cramped up, and now he's wearing two prosthetic devices. I'm not kiddin'! . . . So, Joe, please. Let's get it straight, Pro-Tec makes *Hand-Arbiter,* which is the most revolutionary, and unique prosthetic hand device ever devised by man, basically, a chemo-electronic device, Joe, whereas the others are all—mechanical. There's hell of a difference, guy. You got the press kit, right? . . . It says Pro-Tec. You see the little insignia on the folder cover? An artificial hand holding up the torch? . . . Like the Statue of Liberty, that's right. That's us . . . Okay, Joe? Listen, if you have any other questions, don't hestitate to give a call. Let's have lunch one of these days. If we're going to be working together, we ought to get to know each other, you know what I mean? . . . Okay, so take care, Joe. Talk to you soon . . . Thanks a lot."

Do I know what I'm doing, or do I know what I'm doing? That son of a bitch Frank doesn't know what a gold mine he has in me.

Meanwhile, back in the real world. Waiting for Lacy's call. The trick is to keep busy. There is garbage to take to the town dump, but I'm afraid to leave in case Lacy should call back at any minute. So I decide to rake a few leaves from the lawn. My daughter is up. She knows what has happened, and is walking a careful course between our disapproval of Peter's behavior and loyalty to her brother. She is wise enough to keep a low profile, at least for now, and I admire her for it. *This* monument, anyway, we have crafted right, and it is a salvation.

How is it possible that a brother and sister, so close in age, brought up in identical ways, it would seem, as even-handedly as we could manage it, could turn out so different? It is a mystery, though the problem for me is, I really don't believe in mysteries. What I believe is, there's an answer to everything, and if we don't know the answer, it's only out of ignorance. I, therefore, have to believe that somehow we have failed with Peter. Which, of course, is what makes the whole business so abysmally depressing. It's our fault. This skulking little bastard is off smoking dope, listening to lyrics of some rock group exhorting him to violence, and responding ungratefully to our every effort to help him as interference in his life. And I end up feeling guilty. I'll show him what interference is; he doesn't begin to know yet about interference.

Forty-five mintues after hanging up, Lacy calls back, and my daughter gets me in from the leaves.

"Hello? Mr. Lacy?"

"Yes, hello. Can you hold, please?"

The little shit! Yes, I can hold. I can fandango in the nude, if that's what it will take to give my kid a break.

"I met with the boy's advisor," he says, coming back on.

"Yessir." Breathless.

But, then, he's off again, the mouthpiece half covered as he banters with someone else, in his office. "Tell her—mumble, muffle—Ha, ha—That's all right—muffle, mumble . . . Hello, Mr. Brock?"

"I'm here."

"We're going to send the boy home—for a week—"

I can't hold back a sudden audible choke. "Thank you, sir." I twist my mouth into something halfway between a grin and a grimace at my wife who is standing next to me. Quickly she turns away, and with her back to me, I see that her shoulders are shaking.

"He'll be on probation until Christmas."

"Yessir." I don't want to keep saying "yessir," but I do it, anyway. All the power is with him.

"Can you fetch him this morning?"

"Yessir."

"Good. His teachers are giving him his assignments. I would suggest that he keep up on things during the week."

"Yessir. We'll see to that."

"Good-bye."

"Good-bye, sir."

And it's over. My wife and I are holding each other now, and I am thinking that we are clinging not just to one another, but to the fragility of dear life itself. Until now, I think I have not truly realized just how easy it would be for the life that we know to fall apart. We have succeeded under stress in holding it together this time. Something remedial, and different, will have to be done. We stand there a long time, breathing together rhythmically, softly.

CHAPTER VIII

The picturesque country road on the way up to my son's school takes on the aspect today of a dreary blacktop secondary highway poking through one provincial town after another, each indistinguishable from the other, gas stations, fast-food joints, video outlets, car dealerships and wired overhead traffic signals scattered along the way.

What is troubling is that I don't know precisely how I should act when I see my son. Certainly, I am furious at him. I am also angry (though probably irrationally) at the school. But aside from anger, I am scared. Fearful of the future. I would really just like to walk away from the whole business, but, of course, I cannot do that. I have to be responsible, authoritative, understanding, helpful. Dignified.

I will not fly into a rage—at least, not an uncontrolled rage. If I show anger it will be part of a calculated approach to inspire fear and respect. On the other hand, maybe I should treat the whole thing lightly. "Hey, man, you smoked a little weed, forget it. It's no big deal. Get on with it." Sure. He'd go back, and get busted again, suspended until the year he becomes eligible for Social Security. Or would he? Maybe he would take the attitude, "The old man is right; I gotta get my act together, and start being responsible on my own."

Who the hell knows?

When I arrive at the school, kids are sitting and lying about on the lawn in front of the administration building. I park carefully on the edge of the grass so as not to leave any tire marks. No point in establishing in Lacy's mind a further image of Brock family failed responsibility. A few kids in shirtsleeves fling Frisbees back and forth. An Irish setter prances and races crazily from one group to another. It is one of those New England fall days when you think of football—not the professional kind on television, but the kind you associate with old grads and wives, tailgate picnics and raccoon coats.

I don't have an appointment specifically to see Mr. Lacy, but I stick my head into the outer office to report in to his secretary. She doesn't suggest that I go in to see him, and noting that his door is closed, I don't suggest it, either. She has seen other parents come to fetch their kids, I imagine, and her tone is sympathetic without actually inviting any conversation about it. I am eager for a conversation with someone. Just a few words said to me, like, "Peter's a nice boy. This will probably do him good," or, "Don't feel bad, Mr. Brock, this is very common among boys your son's age." Anything. Just a word of consolation. No. Rather, reassurance. Things will be all right.

Like an angel appearing to answer my prayers, Mrs. Lacy rounds a corner in the corridor outside of her husband's office. I met her the previous spring at a reception at the headmaster's house when they were falling all over themselves to recruit new freshmen. She was pouring tea and continually smiling, and at the time I couldn't help but think that she was mother earth set here to brighten all of our lives. Also, she is under forty, with a perky pair of boobs and a face like Miss Art School Grad

92

Student of five years before, with a no-nonsense-horn-rimmed-glasses serious appearance. She has dark hair swirled in a bun that I figure probably uncoils to at least the crack of her ass.

"Mrs. Lacy," I say by way of intercepting her. I am looking at her with an expression, I know (as a public relations expert) that conveys at least three different impressions that I would like to get across in an instant, namely: I feel sad about my son; but we're a wonderful family; and I know you are an understanding person and will say something that will give me the reassurance I am looking for.

Evidently not reading me closely, and certainly not smiling like last spring, she replies coolly. "Yes?"

"William Brock. I'm here to pick up Peter. You know about it, I guess."

"Yes. Very bad. Bad boy. Not good."

"Yes, well, I think we'll be able to talk a bit of sense to him while he's home."

"I hope so." And lowering her eyelids like a curtain, she squeezes out an "Excuse me," then sidles by in the narrow corridor, and is on her way without another word.

There is a moment when I feel like throwing a body block at her from behind—a spine-snapping clip, if possible—but I suck in a deep breath, and charge off in the opposite direction toward the stairs up to my son's room.

Mounting the stairwell to the second floor is like offering oneself to the gates of hell. I enter a domain of cacophonous blasting, a stereophonic horror of competing rock groups. I have the sense of making my way through the landscape of a Hieronymus Bosch painting—the wail of zithers, the screech of electronics, the thrumming of guitars and percussive crashing, the screams and howling of the demented foisting off their terrorist nightmares onto the world. Is this what I'm paying $11,000 for? How do they study?! No wonder they are all *weedheads;* it would be the only way to survive. Is that clown, Lacy, sucking on a peach, aware of the hell inflicted on the inmates of this institution?

From behind the door of my son's room there emanates a generous contribution to the overall racket. I rap my knuckles on the door, but, of course, make no impression whatsoever on whomever is on the inside. I open the door carefully and stick my head in, not knowing what to expect. There, not my son, but the nerd roommate, is standing with his back to me jiggling his shoulders and wobbling his head in a trance-like state, apparently in some kind of solipsistic accompaniment to the clamor. I approach him quietly (One is intimidated into a humbling silence, as in a church, by the vaulting racket), and tap him on the shoulder. Interrupted in his reverie, he whirls as if to fend off an attack, but seeing me, merely frowns, and reaches down to the desktop which is filled not with books but by his stereo set, and flicks a switch. It is now possible, with the door closed, to be heard (barely) above the roar of other stereo sets from other rooms.

"Hi," I say, shouting. I don't know his name.

The roommate is as uncommunicative as my own son, and I am beginning to think that behind his thick glasses there is the soul of a diabolical criminal. He doesn't speak, but he nods (I think). With a pang of sadness (and envy) I have to acknowledge that nerd or no, the kid is smart enough to use his fan to clear the evidence when he smokes. I have failed to instill into my kid the requisite deviousness.

The roommate doesn't know where my son is. There is no

sign of a packed suitcase, I notice. Possibly he's in the can smoking dope? No, probably skulking about guiltily in the woods, afraid to come out and face me. As well he might be, since I am properly worked up now for a good mean confrontation.

The roommate mumbles something about asking somebody else, and accompanies me into the hall, and toward the stairs, a step or two ahead of me, until we come to two other kids.

Peter is not in the woods hiding; he is out on the lawn playing Frisbee, the kids shout at us. His mother and I have been agonizing over his future for two days, and he's out on the lawn tossing all care away with a flick of the wrist. He will get it now.

Sure enough, there he is, the one with the hair down to his shoulders. Earlier, when I passed by the group of kids on the lawn, I must have disregarded him, thinking he was a girl. *Nobody* wears their hair that long these days, except possibly one of those rampaging slaughterers of Midwest farm families you read about in the *N.Y. Enquirer: Dead sister told him to do it.* There is a moment when the notion grips me to run out onto the lawn, wrestle him to the ground, shave his head, and scream into his ear, "Why the hell aren't you skulking about in the woods like the guilty ratfink punk you are?!" But standing there a minute and watching him racing after that flying disc, leaping gracefully, high into the air, and snagging it backhand in an impossible catch, then whirling, and while still airborne, flinging it back again with perfect direction and speed and stable rotation, I am entranced, my heart stumbles over itself in a sudden catch of admiration. I never could do that, could never even hardly make the damn thing reach the other person.

Where did that particular talent come from? Not from me. From his mother? Hardly. It's *his*, and I can only view it with a kind of amazement.

But that's only for a second. He sees me standing on the edge of the lawn. He flings away the Frisbee one last time, and slouches over.

"Hello," he says, in a tentative tone that suggests he is waiting for a signal from me.

"Hello," I say, echoing his tentativeness. "Are you ready?"

"Yup."

"Where's your bag?"

"I've just got some laundry."

"Where're your clothes?" He is wearing a black T-shirt with some kind of rock group insignia emblazoned across the front and back, and a pair of black corduroy pants and white sneakers. The sneakers are clean, a concession to the school dress code, as are the corduroy pants, Levis not being allowed.

He looks at me, and shrugs. "What clothes? I'll go like this."

"Oh, no, you won't. Pack a jacket! And a necktie!"

"Oh, Dad!"

"Never mind that 'Oh, Dad' stuff! You're suspended for a week. You're going to do things the way I say, and shut up about it!" I've worked up now to the anger that I had intended in the first place, and it feels pretty good. More importantly, it feels *right*, and I can see that he knows better than to challenge it.

"I'll be back in a minute," he says in a low voice.

"Jacket. Necktie. Shoes. Dress shirt. Books, you have homework to do."

"I know!"

"Don't give me that 'I know.' Just do it, and do it *right.*"

He heads toward the dormitory, moving more quickly now, making clear his desire simply to get away from me, head ducked low, shoulders hunched forward, a manner I can't help but recall painfully as identical to my own when I used to skulk away from my father.

"Do you need help?" Calling after him.

"No."

"No, what?"

"No, thanks."

Waiting for him is unpleasant, at least discomfiting, as it is well known around school about his suspension, and I am aware of the kids and passing faculty casting certain curious looks at me. Are they wondering how I am taking all this? The kids, I imagine to be sympathetic to Peter; members of the faculty, judging from the attitude of Mrs. Lacy, are probably disapproving. Any one of them, of course, could have been the fink who nailed Peter smoking in the can. I can't meet their eyes, and I don't want to appear to be avoiding them, either. I remove myself to the car, where I am partially shielded by the tinted glass. My kid gets busted for doing dope, and I end up the one sneaking away guiltily and trying to avoid the stares of the mob.

It is even worse that that. In my mind's eye suddenly I have this vivid fantasy picture of myself being discovered—*found out,* rather—by one of my Amherst classmates (of no particular identity, just a phantom classmate), there, striding purposefully across the lawn on his way to lunch, the guest of Mr. and Mrs. Lacy, bearing a check for $25,000 made out to the school (which is just the first of several gifts he is planning to make; his accountant says it saves him money on taxes).

"Bill Brock! I *thought* that was you behind the tinted glass with your nose stuck into the *New York Times*. You look like you're hiding from somebody, ha, ha. I'm having lunch with Homer and Serena Lacy. Driving the Mercedes over to Bradley Field later to pick up my daughter, Tammy, on her way in from Lichtenstein where she's been visiting her fiancé, the son of the Crown Prince. She got her doctorate last year in Business Administration from M.I.T., and has a job as Undersecretary of War in the Pentagon. I suppose you know that. There's been quite a bit written about her in the *Times*. What's your boy doing?"

"Oh, gosh, he's quite the guy. I'm driving him down from school in the Pontiac for a few days. He has this group of friends he hangs out with at the edge of the parking lot in front of the Grand Union. They smoke dope and drink beer out of paper bags."

Mercifully, my son arrives before I am actually discovered by any old classmates. He throws some kind of khaki duffle bag in the back, which, I presume contains his blazer and necktie rolled up in a ball, and climbs in the front with me, pointing his face straight ahead.

"Buckle your seat belt," I say.

He complies, not quite daring to give me the contemptuous look that no doubt he feels the command deserves.

It's some joyful ride. We sit in silence, rolling along the country road beside the Housatonic. For him, silence is probably a mercy. For me, it is something I can barely endure. What can I say to him? I don't really want to be angry at him. In fact, after a certain point, I begin to feel silly, vulgar, keeping up what is, for me, by now, a charade. What I really want to do is find out what the hell is the matter with him, and why he is screwing up his own and everybody else's life.

"Do you know that they were going to kick you out until Christmas?" I ask him, at last.

"They wouldn't do that," he replies.

"They were doing it! I practically had to beg Lacy—I did beg him—to give you another chance."

"Lacy's an idiot."

"Don't say that!" Although, come to think of it, the kid may be right. Possibly he has insights deeper than we give him credit for. "Why do you say that?"

"He just is."

"I'm sorry. That's not good enough. You got caught smoking dope. What do you expect him to do, congratulate you, and ask you over for tea?"

"I don't mean that."

"Well, you shouldn't have been smoking dope. I sent you to this school to get you away from that kind of stuff, and what you do, you bring your dope with you—you know better than that—and start perverting the other kids."

"I'm not perverting anybody. They're all high all the time."

"Well, they didn't get caught! You must have been doing more than they were."

"No."

"Peter, for Christ sake, why are you wrecking things for yourself? Don't you want to—survive? Do you want to go on to college and make something of your life?"

"Sure, I want to make something of my life. I don't know about college."

"You have to go to college, if you're going to get anywhere."

"I don't know if college will help me get to where I want to go."

"Where is it that you want to go? I mean, I think it's wonderful that you're beginning to think about these things."

"I don't know yet. I know I don't want to be a businessman."

Despite the fact that this is an obvious attempt to disassociate himself from me, I am not displeased. "Good! What would you say if I told you I don't necessarily want you to be a businessman? The question is, What do you want to be?" I remember with a shudder that the last time I asked him he said he was thinking of becoming a stunt man.

"I don't know exactly. I have this feeling—I've just had it a little while. I don't know, I'd like to do something—*important.*"

Again, that catch in the chest, as when he was leaping and flinging the Frisbee. I wrote that to my father from Paris, the exact same words, that I wanted to do something—important. How can I make him see how much alike we are? "That's *wonderful,*" I say. Though immediately I wonder if he believes that I mean it when I say it. In truth, I have this moment of doubt as to whether or not I believe it myself. It was wonderful when I was young and wanted to change the world with a few well-chosen words on paper. Do I believe it's quite as wonderful that he wants to do something similar?

"I want to get educated," he volunteers further. "But this school—I mean, Lacy may not be an idiot—but he and I—we don't see things the same way."

"It's the wrong school?" I feel a sense of panic rising.

"I dunno. He wants everyone to be a certain way."

100

I glance over at him, at the black rock-and-roll T-shirt. "Is that so terrible?"

"Terrible? I dunno. We're different, is all."

I find myself rushing in. "You gotta finish the year, kid. Eleven thousand bucks. It's already plunked down."

"I'll finish."

We don't say anything for a few miles as I dog the tail of some contractor poking along at twenty-five miles an hour in his pickup truck with a bumper sticker, "If you don't like it here, get your a--out over there."

"You know what I think," I say, at last. "You want to do something important with your life, I think you're an idealist. Do you know what that is?"

"Yeah, I think so."

"The world is better because of people like you." It is an opportunity to put a bright face on the disturbing events of the last couple of days. "This country was founded on idealism. People wanted to make a better world. They did it, too."

"Not for the Indians, they didn't."

"I'm not talking about Indians!" He always has this annoying way of interrupting a train of thought, even when you're trying to give him a compliment. Youth never understands. But I don't care, for the moment. Certainly I do not need to win an argument with my son. We are *talking*. This has never happened before. "Do other kids feel the same way?" I ask him.

"About what?"

"About what we're talking about—doing something—important."

"Some do."

"You mean, kids you've met already at school?"

"No, not them. Not at school."

"Who, then?"

"Some of the kids in the park."

"You mean, near the Grand Union?!"

"Yeah, some of them."

"They don't think about *anything*!"

"Yeah, they do. You don't know them."

"They're losers! Dropouts! Criminals."

"They're not criminals. They just don't see much place anywhere for them."

"I'll say they don't."

"But they have some good ideas."

"No, they don't. What kind of ideas?"

"I don't know. A lot of things that are crazy they see pretty clear."

"Not those guys. They don't see anything. They don't believe in anything—except maybe complete destruction."

"Maybe that's all there is."

"Wonderful! Have you thought about becoming a terrorist?"

He turns to look at me for the first time. "What are you getting so hyper about?"

"I can't stand this negativism! One minute you want to do something important. The next minute you're ready to tear everything down."

"Maybe it's the same thing."

"Yeah, yeah, sure. Give me a break, will you? What are you talking about? The bomb? That's not going to happen. That's a cop-out, and you know it. What are you saying, we're all doomed?"

"It doesn't necessarily have to be the bomb."

102

"Well, what, then? What, *aliens?*"

Because he does not reply immediately, but instead lets escape what sounds like a small snort, I am obliged at last to glance over at him out of the corner of my eye. He is smiling to himself, but it is a smile that, in fact, I do not like at all, one that has not a touch of mirth in it, an expression that is totally unfamiliar to me, one that I have never seen before in this face that I have spent so many hours observing in so many various attitudes at so many various times, and until this moment have always felt I knew so well.

"Maybe just ourselves," he says at last.

It is strangely disturbing. Disturbing. "I don't know what that means," I say. "How?"

He scrunches down in his seat so that the seat belt crosses between his neck and chin. "I don't know," he says.

CHAPTER IX

This is no vacation my son is on. His being home is a punishment, and I expect him to do penance. I also expect him to keep up with his studies, to behave respectfully in the presence of his mother, sister and myself, and to give careful attention to his manner and appearance.

All of this I outline to him in the presence of his mother in our country kitchen/family area upon arrival home just before lunch. He had thought that he would go over to the high school in the early afternoon and meet some of his less objectionable pals, *not* the dropout gang that hangs out at the Grand Union, he assures us, but some of the blander louts who appear from time to time, usually about the time we are sitting down to dinner, scratching at the pane of the kitchen slider. His idea being, I suppose, to inspire a bit of awe swaggering about and regaling the admiring crowd with a recounting of his suspension, not neglecting to elaborate, of course, on the hilarious spectacle of his old man who went ape for awhile, but everything's cool now, so come on over to the room tonight, and we'll listen to some tunes, yeah!

Yeah, well, you can forget that.

"You're home for a week on suspension, kid. Don't make plans."

"Oh!"

And there's more.

"Every morning—at eight sharp—I want you at the dining room table, studying. Until 12:30. You can have a glass of milk at ten."

"Dad!"

"Lunch is over at 1:30 at which time you start painting the house. The outside."

"What?!"

"Which means, you start by scraping off the old peeled paint."

"Oh, my God!"

"And I want it done right. You can stop at 5:30. A glass of milk at three. I'll check your work when I get home."

"Yeah, great."

"And please keep your mouth shut until I'm finished." And I give him a hard look, catching and holding his eye. Does he want to challenge me? He looks away.

Deciding upon all of this has not come easy to me, but it's been forming in little bits and pieces—all during the previous sleepless night, and on the way up to school, and during the long silent periods between our discussion on the way back. I'm on a roll, as they were saying just a day or two ago in Las Vegas, and it feels good.

"That gives you an hour and a half to relax, then freshen up, and get ready for dinner. Shirt and tie. Jacket."

"Oh!"

"If you have anybody you want to see, they can come to the house. Between 5:30 and seven. You do not go out. After dinner, you study until 10:30. You can have—"

"—A glass of milk. Gee, thanks a lot."

"Do you want not to see anybody?"

Sheepishly. "No."

"Then, keep quiet. Those are the rules while you are home. Any deviation, and—" It occurs to me that I really haven't carried my thinking to the point of knowing how in the world I will enforce any of this should he look me in the eye, and say, "Fuck off, Dad." I can't *spank* him. There aren't many privileges left to take away from him. "—There'll be—consequences. You'll be sorry." A little bit of family brinksmanship there.

I look over at Annie. She has remained silent during all of this. It matters not that I wish she would jump in and take a more aggressive position in support of me. She merely looks away, and I am not sure, in fact, that she even agrees with me. At least, she hasn't contradicted me in front of Peter. I wonder if he is weighing her reaction, as I am. Which, if he is, he may be thinking my words have no teeth. In which case, I am up the creek without a paddle, and not even with a prayer book.

"That's all," I say, carrying off the rather uncertain threat with a gruff dismissal. "You know what you have to do. It's 12:30 now. Grab a sandwich, and get busy scraping."

"Can I put my bag in my room first?"

"Yes."

Without another word, he pushes his chair back and rises, making his unhappiness clear by a certain amount of noisiness about it (like his mother, I'm afraid), at the same time taking care not to allow his rebellious feelings too much free reign, and slouches out of the room.

I am rather pleased. I keep forgetting that for fifteen years he has been accustomed to viewing me as absolute authority in this domain, and though he is certainly chomping at the bit now to challenge my position, there is a residue of power that remains with me and still commands respect, simply out of habit. How many corrupt duchies and island dictatorships have been maintained in times of rebelliousness by just such habitual ways on the part of the subject populations?

It would be nice now, I am thinking, if my wife would smile, wink knowingly at me, give me a little pat on the shoulder ("Good job, Bill"), rise from her chair, and slither gracefully over to the fridge and bring out a nice light lunch for us of iced shrimp, fresh oysters, a country paté, and sliced garden ripe tomatoes, the last of the season, with a sprinkling of fresh basil leaves on top. But I have an unerring sense in advance that it won't happen that way. Instead, she remains seated, and that means she wants to initiate a conversation. Or rather, it means that she is waiting for me to initiate a conversation. She will sit there all afternoon and say nothing until I ask her what the trouble is. I have told her that she does this, but she denies it. Nevertheless, there she is, waiting. And, of course, somehow I knew she would just sit there. Because the whole time I was talking, she was giving off these negative vibrations that both Peter and I were picking up on. Which, as a matter of fact, from my point of view, we could have done very well without. *I* don't know whether I'm on solid ground or not with my son. Well, I guess she's going to tell me, isn't she.

"Well?" I begin. But I know as soon as I say it that that is too indefinite to get her started. "What do you think?" I add.

"About what?" Now she rises, and goes to the fridge, not slithering, however. Rather, slouching. The body English is painfully obvious. In another moment she plunks down on the table a platter of cold left-over lamb immured in an island of congealed gray fat.

"About what I said to Peter."

"Well, you said what you had to say."

"But do you agree?"

"I think he should be on a schedule, yes."

"And if he deviates from it?"

"You shouldn't make threats."

There it is. I knew it. "How else am I going to get him to stay in line?"

"You wouldn't want to have to do something you'd be sorry for later."

As usual, she has put her finger directly on the problem. I don't know what I would do if I were to find that there's no controlling him. "We can't just let him run all over us, you know. I'm trying—forgive me—I'm trying to maintain a little bit—just a little tiny bit—of dignity—if you'll pardon the expression." My voice is going British again.

"Can the shit, will you?" she says.

"Don't say that."

"Well, talk sense."

"I am talking sense!" Though I am not absolutely certain whether I am or not. In any case, there's no winning with her. "I'm going out and rake leaves," I say.

"Have a piece of lamb," she says.

"I'll have an apple," I say. Which I take, polishing it on the front of my jacket, as I leave the room.

Raking leaves, I am thinking, is a lot like trying to be a father. There's this enormous mess spread all about on the ground, and it is up to you, singlehandedly to attack it and set the yard right again. And even as you pile the leaves onto the tarpaulin to drag them into the nearby woods (which is not even my property, as a matter of fact, but nobody has ever complained yet), more leaves are swirling down, threatening to bury you. That means a week later going through the whole exercise all over again, and then one final time again. And, still, you never get them all, anyway.

No one helps me rake, of course. My wife is pushing a vacuum cleaner around the living room, most likely feeling at the moment that she is being taken advantage of. My daugher suddenly appears bounding down the front steps, rushing off somewhere.

"Want to help me rake leaves?" I say at her, trying to conceal the irony in my voice, knowing full well what the answer will be. I remember when she was little she used to help. Well, at least, she kept me company, she and her brother disturbing the neat piles I had made by burying each other and then bursting forth like Proteus rising from the sea.

"Gotta meet Missy!" she calls, waving cheerfully, and passing by. "Doing a good job, Dad."

"Oh, yeah." And she is gone.

The alternative to doing this would be to go to the office, but since it is already two o'clock, and it would be close to three before I could get in, it makes no sense.

Chet Dowd is home today, on R & R between flights. He, too, has decided to attack the leaves in his yard, and our two heads bob up and surface on opposite sides of the hedge between our properties.

"How ya doin', Chet?!"

"How ya doin', Bill?!"

I could tell him that I flew home with him on the same

110

plane last night. Instead, I say, "When you're finished doing your yard, you can start on mine, Chet." Ha, ha.

"What?" he says. A car has just gone by the front of the house, drowning out my words.

"I say, it's a hell of a job, eh?"

"Raking leaves."

"Yeah."

"Yeah. Awful." He interrupts his work for a moment, standing the rake on end beside him, bringing to mind for an instant the Grant Wood painting. "Did I see Peter come home with you a little while ago?"

He doesn't miss much. "Yes. Home for a little R & R."

"No kiddin'?" He cocks his head and sucks the meat of his cheek between his teeth. "When did you take him up there to that school? Sunday?"

"Yeah. Yeah, he's home for a couple of days." Let him wonder about it.

"How's he like it there?"

"Crazy about it. Yeah. Really likes it a lot."

"Gee, that's great."

"Yeah, we're pretty pleased." I look down at where I've been raking and note that I have broken through the turf, and am scratching up dirt. "See ya later," I say, and make a point of bending down to clean the end of the rake, lowering my body from the waist, submerging below the top of the hedge.

He'll find out. Wait'll his kid becomes a teen-ager.

Back to the raking. I ought to sleep well tonight. I'm still on jet lag. I probably slept two to three hours last night, and on top of that, I'm emotionally drained. Feeling so alone. Boy, let's face it, being 50 is no fun. Physically I feel okay. This raking, for example, doesn't tire me out. I still get that gleam in the eye when the old lady comes out of the shower and slips on a pair of panties and sidles by me to get to the dresser for a bra, boobies jiggling, almost as if they were put there for the sole purpose of bringing on that first twitch in the joint over which I have no control, and which never fails to amaze me. I *love* to grab her then. When she's nice and warm and smells of hair rinse and fresh towelled skin. As often as not, she'll say, it's not a good time. And just as often, I ask, Why not? Well, she just got out of the shower. That's the *best* time. We'll be late. So what? Not now. So I pull on my Jockey shorts, bending the head of my dick and tucking it down under, taming it into place, and a few minutes later we're dressed and ready to go to wherever it is we don't want to be late for, me vowing to myself, however, to get her later that night, though knowing full well that we'll both be too tired then. (So being 50 *does* make a difference!) It usually works out that I catch her in the morning, most often on a Sunday morning, putting out that first tentative hand on the hip, and waiting for whatever reaction I'm going to get. I leave it there for minute or two, and if there isn't a big heave and production of rolling away, I know I'm in. A little slow movement of the hand here and there, and up to the boobies, and on her part just the slightest bit of settling into me, and then the kissing. And she reaches out to me. Pretty predictable stuff, but it still works, and I like it, and usually I can make her *holler.*

Still, after two children, and twenty years of living together, it is not as easy to arouse my wife sexually as it once was.

Though there are those who would disagree, I believe that romance is more important to women in lovemaking than it is to men. And I sometimes wonder, how romantic can a woman feel living with that same old breadwinner, that lout who day after day slouches home from the office, and plops himself down in the country kitchen/family area and watches TV while she makes supper. She doesn't really believe in romance any more, and maybe he doesn't either, but since it's more important to her nature to have it, it is his job to construct a facsimile of it now and then, and to fool her, as she wants to be fooled, into believing, one more time, that romance is alive, just for a little while, anyway. That's why it's so tentative at first on a Sunday morning in bed.

Time flies with the leaves as these thoughts fill my mind. The yard is almost finished. *Where* is that no-account son of mine? I have not heard the aluminum ladder banging, as I think I should have if he were to have put it up already against the house. I don't want to be obvious about looking around the side of the house to check it out; that would tend to undo the authority that I have established. So it's a feeling somewhat like being a housebreaker when I maneuver myself around to the side next to the driveway, scratching at some of the new leaves that have fallen since I was over this way five minutes ago. And, by golly! There he is! Up on the ladder, two and a half stories up, peeling paint with a scraper, hanging out to the side, one leg free in the air.

"Move the ladder over! Don't lean out too far!" I call.

"It's all right!" he calls back.

I keep forgetting that he's the stunt man. I rake there for a few minutes, sneaking looks up at him from time to time. Why? Not to check on him. Why? To admire him. His grace—at scraping. Oh, come on! But it's true, I can't take my eyes off him, up there, leaning out from the ladder. You can't get him to move the ladder over. He has to do it his own way, and he does it, yes, with grace. It is like watching him with the Frisbee. He is his own man, and he brings to this new task, to him now made tolerable as a feat of derring-do, a beauty, to me, that is like, yes, a poem.

The little bastard. Will he learn anything from this latest experience at school? Can I teach him? Which way will he go?

For the moment, I suppose I will be content merely if he doesn't fall off the ladder and break his neck.

CHAPTER X

Another day, another dollar. Here I am crawling along in a line of traffic at eight a.m., caught in the morning rush into corporate Stamford. Since this is white-collar country in which business of the day officially begins at nine a.m., one might think that an hour early at eight o'clock I'd have it all to myself, but these days only the secretaries get in as late as nine. The rest of us managers pull in anywhere from seven o'clock on so as to get a little something done before the phones start ringing. Twenty years ago corporate people who lived in Fairfield County were obliged to get up at six o'clock, early enough to catch a commuter train into Manhattan to be at work by 9:15, or more likely, by 9:30. Then the corporations moved to the suburbs. Anybody who thought this would mean another hour's sleep in the morning quickly got disabused of that. The office officially is open for business at nine, but with guys like Mac McDougall getting in at seven every morning, and Frank usually at his desk by eight, the rest of us find ourselves still getting up at the old time, but spending the extra train ride hour now at our desks. Somebody knew something about productivity when they started the corporate move to the suburbs.

The only time I ever listen to the radio is in the car, and I have it on now, the AM waveband with some "talk radio" host interviewing an author of a book on how parents can deal with the problems of teen-age drug addiction. The author is solemn and single-mindedly determined to plug his book, while the talk show host, fearing that his audience may not be ready at this early hour for such heavy stuff, keeps interrupting with silly comments and jokes. Personally, I wish he'd shut up, as we parents need all the help we can get. I reach into the glove compartment, driving with one hand, and fish around for a pencil and scrap of paper on which to write down the name of the book.

There is a five-minute news summary at 8:15. A fire in Brooklyn, arson suspected. Another flare-up of military activity in Central America. Guerrilla rebels have overrun three towns, with 50 government troops killed and six civilian government employees taken hostage. I can't make out whether these anti-government rebels are good anti-government rebels or bad anti-government rebels. They are either Salvadorans or Somozans or Sandinistas, and depending on which, are either financed and supported by our government, or are under attack by forces financed and supported by our government. I try to keep current on these things, but it is true, it is not easy, I have to make a conscious effort through a trick of memory association I have worked out to clarify who is who. Actually, I'm getting sick of all of them, but they don't go away.

It is only after the commercial break that it becomes clear that these rebels are bad rebels, because a bulletin from the State Department has just been released and sent out over the newswires stating that two of the civilian hostages are Americans, described as economic advisors, who happened to be

116

directing government fire at the time, and the rebels holding them are described as terrorists.

In the time that it has taken to make a pitch for a local savings bank, the Central America news story has suddenly turned serious. And before I reach Stamford, there are more bulletins released, the last one stating that the Pentagon has ascertained that the raids on the three Central American towns were designed specifically for the purpose of capturing the Americans, the attack now being referred to as a kidnapping, and that the action was conducted on direct orders from a terrorist faction with ties to Communist Cuba. An hour ago a note was delivered to Cuba through the Soviet ambassador in Washington, the contents of which are not known, but are rumored to be a statement of intention to send in American F-111 jet planes to bomb several mountain villages believed to be guerrilla strongholds. A press conference is scheduled by the Secretary of State for ten a.m.

The talk show host, following the newscast, has moved quickly, now promising us a phone interview with a retired military strategy expert living in California (where it is 5:15 a.m.). Apparently they have given the teen-age drug addiction author the hook, as we do not hear from him again, although he was cut off in the midst of a sentence just before the newsbreak. I pull the car over to the curb to hear what the military strategy expert has to say, as I have arrived at the entrance to the subterranean parking garage underneath the building where Pro-Tec has its offices, and once inside, there is no radio reception. The military strategy expert comes on, sounding as though he's been wide awake for hours and has had time to figure it all out, and says that a bombing of guerrilla occupied villages makes a lot of sense, as it is now possible to pinpoint targets so as to hit only guerrillas, and not civilians. The talk show host, who a few moments before was giggling and making silly jokes about teen-age drug addiction, is now warning that if we don't wipe out this spreading cancer south of our border, we all may be obliged in a few short years to defend freedom at the steps of our own homes. I pull out from the curb, and head toward the entrance to the parking garage. I've got news for the talk show host. I already have at the steps of my own house my own terrorist, who right now, hopefully, is scraping paint off the side of it, which may be the best antidote in the world to the further proliferation of whatever kind of hideous growth is spreading within him these days.

There are three levels to the subterranean parking garage, and you park your car wherever you can find a space; at this hour of the day they are fairly plentiful. One advantage of an underground parking lot is you never have to worry about getting wet if it's raining. You go directly from your car to an elevator and up. All you have to do is remember where in that vast smoggy underground cavern you parked, especially remembering the level.

Stepping out of the vast damp echoing concrete garage into the carpeted elevator with its morning Muzak and the smell of makeup and perfume somehow gives me the sense that I am about to visit Disneyland, except that almost immediately the blood starts to flow a bit faster, and in another moment, as we approach the fifth floor where the Pro-Tec offices are located, I have a new sensation, not unlike, I imagine, what a football linebacker must feel when he's on the sidelines and getting ready to go in. Who knows, the first ball buster you meet on the floor might be Diana Payne-Pignatelli.

Today, however, it is not Diana, nor the other front-line

118

bruisers who are on the field. Having just finished up in Las Vegas the previous day, the team probably got in late last night. That means they're entitled to an extra half hour or so of rest in bed, and they'll be coming in a bit later this morning. All except Frank, of course, our coach, who you can be certain will be in the office—in fact, is there, as I enter, already conferring with Mac McDougall. They are in Mac's office, jackets off; you can see them through the glass walls of Mac's office, behind the potted rubber plant.

One of the unspoken but nonetheless graven precepts of corporate life at Pro-Tec is that no matter what one's private feelings, it is absolutely essential that everyone be able to work closely and cooperatively together for the better good of the company. At least, there should be the appearance of objectivity and cooperation. If it should become too apparent that two management level employees cannot work together, one or the other must yield, which usually means one gets fired. Or at least, demoted. It's why I am always smiling and simpering around Diana.

Because no one knows the rules better than Tony Passanante and Morrie Glick, they both are eager to patch up the "little misunderstanding" that took place three nights ago during the Wayne Newton "concert." And the manner in which this is to be accomplished, I am informed at 9:30 a.m. today by none other than Diana Payne-Pignatelli, is that Morrie and Tony would like to have lunch together, if I will accompany them, or rather, in a facesaving maneuver, if I will issue invitations to them both to lunch with me. Diana spent the whole day yesterday negotiating between the two men. As much as she can't stand Tony Passanante, she knows that Morrie must have a working cordial relationship with him.

"Diana, these guys hate each other. They won't go to lunch together," I say to her.

"They will. I've already arranged for it," she replies. "Please, Brock," she says. I could kill her when she presumes to address me by my last name. She must be feeling very sure of her position these days. It always makes me want to call her Payne-Pignatelli. Which is ridiculous. Or just plain Piggy. Which, you never know, maybe could get me fired. Of course, it does occur to me that if I handle this with aplomb, and possibly win her good graces, at the rate she is progressing within the company, I may be building up some goodwill that I may need one of these days, say, during a new housecleaning.

"I don't mind inviting them," I say. "They can only say no."

"They won't say no," she assures me. "I've made a reservation for the three of you, in your name at The Skytop Club."

"Who's paying?"

"Put it on your American Express, and charge it to the company."

"I can't do that. What if Mac questions it?"

"It's an investment in the future, Brock," she says. And she looks me in the eye, the bitch, as if to say what I already know. She is on the way up, and I am comfortably perched where I am. And the time will come when my perch will remain more secure when a new team comes in if I make a little investment now. "You can find a way of burying it," she adds.

Is this what dignity comes to? Should I say, "I'll take my chances, Diana. So long. *You* invite them to lunch." That would be a hot one.

"Okay, Di," I say. "Good for you. I wouldn't have thought anyone could have brought these two guys together."

"It wasn't easy," she says.

And in another one of my inelegant fantasies, I suddenly picture her getting a commitment from Morrie just at the point of orgasm.

"Go to lunch with Passanante, or take it out, Glick." I wonder if she calls him by his last name when they're making it.

And how did she persuade Tony? Oh, my, could she have volunteered for his raffle, after all? Jesus, I really don't have any dignity.

I have to invite these guys to lunch, but I also have to earn my keep. The mail has been piling up for three days—four, actually, if you count last Saturday. It's stacked in a precarious pile on my desk. I have the feeling you could take all of it, and drop it into the wastebasket, and it would not matter. Nevertheless, I have to go through it, marking it appropriately so that Jinny will be able to file it (when she gets a chance, after she has filed Tony's stuff) after which it will remain forever unlooked at again. It will take a good hour to go through it all, and then I can get down to replying to some of it, and after that I will make some phone calls to some of the press guys who attended the Pro-Tec press conference, and pick up some vibrations as to how bad they really thought it was, and whether or not that will actually affect the kind of publicity exposure we will get.

At ten o'clock Annie telephones to tell me that my father called a few minutes before to ask how Peter is doing at school.

"What'd you tell him?"

"He sort of caught me off balance. I told him he was home for a few days."

"Oh, no! Jesus!"

"Well, he wanted Peter's phone number. I was afraid he'd go ahead and call the school."

"You should have told him they don't give out the phone numbers of the kids."

"I didn't think fast enough. Anyway, he's going to see Peter Saturday."

"What?!"

"Have you forgotten? It's your Dad's birthday Saturday. We promised to go up and see him."

"You'll forgive me if I forgot. I just happen to have about fifteen million things on my mind."

"I'm not criticizing, but I'm saying Peter will be with us when we go up. We can't leave him at home alone. At least, I don't think we should."

"I agree on that. Did you tell my father why Peter was home?"

"I said there was a misunderstanding. Peter would be going back on Sunday."

"What'd he say to that?"

"Nothing."

"Nothing?"

"Something like, 'Oh, fine.' Or something. He doesn't really want to know."

"True." My old man doesn't need any bad news. I'm on the road there myself.

Back into the phone, to my wife. "Okay. So we'll face up to it. Anything else? Is Peter studying?"

"Yes. He's hard at it."

"Good. I'll see you later. Let's have a light supper. I'm having lunch at The Skytop Club."

"Oh my goodness. Don't drink too much."

"I won't."

"Who's all going?"

"I'll tell you later." And we hang up.

At ten o'clock most work on the bullpen floor stops until 10:15 during which time all secretaries and bullpen denizens repair to the cafeteria for a break. The cafeteria is a sunless interior room with formica tables and chairs, a small refrigerator, a sink, an electric stove and a microwave oven. A concessionaire appears every morning at ten and every afternoon at three with coffee. If you want a donut, you purchase it from the vending machine, which also carries sandwiches that can be heated up in the microwave. This idea of a fifteen-minute break was conceived by Frank who couldn't stand the thought of employees sipping coffee or sodas at their desks, and possibly spilling on the beige carpeting. As a consequence, from ten to 10:15 should a customer want to reach a line manager or customer service representative, no one is around, they are all drinking coffee. This happens at least once a day, and probably has resulted in the loss of a sale a day for the past two years from irate customers who have hung up in disgust.

At 10:30, with everyone refreshed and back at their desks, I wander into Morrie's office to ask him to lunch. Morrie, of course, knows what I'm up to, and doesn't beat about the bush. "If that son of a bitch even mentions Vegas—" he starts in.

"We'll stay away from the subject, Morrie," I promise him.

Tony greets me with a big smile when I wander into his office a couple of minutes later, after having stopped at the water cooler on the way so as not to appear to have come directly from Morrie.

"Brock, you big turd. How the hell are ya?"

"What time did you get in last night?"

"Late, man. Late. I'm exhausted."

"It was a good show," I say. "Your guys were on the ball."

"What happened at the press conference?" he asks. "Did I see a lot of guys leaving?"

"A few."

"I got a call from one of my salesmen who says one of the magazines is going to run a big feature on the hand job."

"No kiddin'? You did?"

"No shit. This guy said it was a big deal."

"Good. I'm not surprised. Most of the editors are pretty loyal to me."

Tony grins again. "Brock, you shit, you always take credit for yourself, don't you."

"Listen, if I don't give myself credit nobody else will."

"No, you deserve credit. You're okay."

I love hearing it, and maybe now is a good time to mention lunch. He knows why I'm there, anyway, and is just waiting.

"Sure, hell, yes," he says. "No hard feelings. It was just a little misunderstanding. Over a broad. It's unimportant. We all had a few drinks."

"I wouldn't even mention Vegas, if I were you," I say. "Let's go on from here. How's your golf game? Have you been playing much lately? Morrie likes golf."

"Cut it out, Brock. Have you ever seen him play?"

"I don't play, myself."

"I mean, it's a fuckin' joke."

"Really? I thought he was pretty good. He's got a nice set of clubs. I saw 'em in the trunk of his car one day."

"He swings at the fuckin' ball, and actually misses it."

"No, he doesn't."

"He *does,* man."

"Well, don't talk about Vegas, is all."

"Don't worry about it. We'll talk about something. It's unimportant. Pick me up at 12:30."

"Okay," I say.

And not knowing quite why I am in the midst of all this, I go back to my desk, and start making some of my phone calls to guarantee that our hand job will get a fair shake in the next month's editions of the leading trade publications.

CHAPTER XI

At 12:30 I pick up Tony, and the two of us wander over to Morrie's office. Diana is in with Morrie, leaning over his shoulder looking over some papers with him. While I stand in attendance in the doorway, Tony holds himself a few feet back, concentrating his gaze on the ceiling, as though viewing for the first time the dome of the Sistine Chapel. Morrie keeps us waiting maybe only a minute or two, just long enough to let us know that dignity demands a certain obeisance; not so long, however, as to provoke us to say, "Fuck it," and stalk off to the elevator without him.

Diana slips by me in the doorway, without a comment, and Morrie looks up then and makes quite a point of being surprised to see us there.

"Oh, there are *three* of us?" he says. I could kill him.

Morrie leads the way to the elevator, with me close behind, and Tony following me. With me in the center, there is a good chance they won't get to strangle each other before we get outside the door. We take the elevator to the top (tenth floor) to The Skytop Club, one more amenity within the building complex that obviates any need to go outside for services. Within the same complex of buildings you can also shop for anything from fur coats to motorcycles, and there are fourteen other restaurants available, ranging from stand-up hotdog stands to a steak pub or two. Membership in The Skytop Club is limited to executives, whose companies pay annually for the privilege of being overcharged at lunch. But it is a convenient and pleasant dining room for fancy entertaining, and it provides a nice view of downtown Stamford, and of Long Island Sound.

Directly off the elevator there is a receptionist at a desk, one of those quite stylish divorced or early-widowed ladies of about 50, with frosted hair, who has been reduced somewhat from former elevated circumstances. She smiles graciously by way of greeting. She knows us, and doesn't ask to see my Pro-Tec membership card.

To keep her company, she has a portable radio turned down low, and I catch a snatch of an earnest voice going on about the hostage situation south of the border.

"Anything happening?" I ask her.

"Isn't it terrible," she says, and shudders and grimaces, as though having missed an easy putt.

"Any more developments?"

She shrugs. "They're calling for some kind of negotiations."

"Who is?"

She shrugs again. "I don't know. I didn't get it all." She smiles at me, and I smile back.

We get a pretty good table by a window, which only costs me a five-dollar tip, and we all order martinis.

The booze has the desired effect of loosening us up, rather than of unleashing old resident hostilities. Tony is loud, and Morrie, attempting to be suave, is only mildly unctuous, the gleam in both of their eyes wary like two Sumo wrestlers. My role in all of this is to act as a sort of referee, or to be more accurate, interlocutor. That is, they are doing all the talking, back and forth, but all comments are directed at me. As, for example:

TONY: "D'jew see that Jets game Sunday, Brock?"

MORRIE: "They sacked O'Brien, what, five times?"

TONY: "Six!"

MORRIE: "He needs protection."

TONY: "Defense is good. That new kid—. Whatsis name? You know who I mean, Brock?"

MORRIE: "Madison."

TONY: "That's the guy. Dwayne."

It goes on like this, the two of them discussing personnel, strategy, scoring odds, locker room gossip, every conceivable aspect of the game, all comments and questions directed at me, who knows nothing of any of it, and have nothing to contribute as they go on and on about it. I can only conclude it is a way for them to discourse without actually saying anything.

As we go for a second martini and order shrimp cocktails, we move on to golf, Morrie knowing enough about the game to carry on an exchange with Tony, at the same time wisely deferring to Tony's superior knowledge and prowess.

All three of us claim to be trying to lose weight, so after the martinis and the shrimp cocktails are taken away, we limit ourselves to one bottle between us of chilled Meurseault (which Tony and I both insist that Morrie order), and three Veal Piccate's with a salad rather than a pasta side dish. Whether or not we will have dessert hangs in the balance, but the pastries here are very good.

There is no mention or even hint of the altercation at Caesar's Palace three days before. The object of this luncheon, it is clear to everyone, is not to discuss deep-seated hostilities. Possibly such a discussion between these two could end in tables being overturned. Rather, the reconciliation is to be in the form of pretending that nothing ever happened, thereby proving to themselves, and to the world, that it is possible to get through a luncheon together without actually strangling one another.

After the main course is cleared away and the dessert tray is wheeled around, we all three of us decide to abandon our dieting for the day, Morrie choosing the strawberry cheesecake, Tony deciding on the Black Forest chocolate torte, and I ordering the Paris-Brest. Three expressos, Morrie saying, "Make mine a double."

By this time we have exhausted pretty much our reserve of conversational subjects—football, baseball, golf, and the upcoming basketball season. Tennis, the only game I know anything about, there isn't much to comment on, except for Tony to volunteer that "McEnroe doesn't take shit from nobody."

And so, there comes a moment, as we await delivery of the coffee, when there is a longer than usual silence among us, occasioning Morrie and me to follow Tony's example by facing out through the expanse of window and surveying the view of downtown Stamford and Long Island Sound. Which, to my mind, is something you can only do for so long a period of time without beginning to feel a little self-conscious, so I venture to ask what they think about the hostage situation.

"Fuck," says Tony.

"Yeah," Morrie says.

"Fuckers gonna get it this time," Tony adds.

"They're talking about sending in F-111's," I say.

"Yeah, fuck 'em up the ass," Tony says. It occurs to me that Tony rates international politics on the same level as one of his raffles.

"You should be Secretary of State," I say to him.

"You got it, babe," he says. "My first act in office. Drop two on Havana."

"That's a laugh riot," I say. "You know what they say the best thing to do is in case of a nuclear attack?"

"What's that?" says Morrie.

"Put your head down between your legs. Then kiss your ass goodbye."

Tony roars. Morrie looks puzzled for a moment, then smiles thinly. After which, he says, "Be serious, you guys. We gotta go in, right?"

"They're talking about negotiating," I say. "According to the hostess."

"Fuck negotiating," Tony says.

"Tony, Mr. Secretary, if you don't mind," I say, "I'm not ready yet to cash in my chips. I'd like to see Paris again before I die."

"Why? You worried they gonna bomb us back, or something?" Tony nudges Morrie. "Brock's afraid they'll come up with a fuckin' Piper Cub, and drop a stick of dynamite on the capitol."

"We keep messing around down there," I say. "What the hell are we doing there?"

"Well, we *have* to be there," Morrie says with gravity. He looks around circumspectly over his shoulders. "It's probably not nice to say this, but it's the truth, the people down there, they're not really quality, do you know what I mean? I mean, if we weren't watching over them, there's no telling what it would be like down there." He is patient in explaining it to me. "The question is, fundamentally, do we stand for anything, or don't we? There's a question of human dignity involved, too. Do we stand for that, or don't we?"

I find myself quickly turning away from Morrie's gaze. I am, of course, the wrong person for him to be asking. I have no idea in the world what we stand for. I mean, I agree, I think, I believe in the same things, but do I even know what dignity calls for in this situation?

"I just question whether we have to blow up everybody, every time there's a problem," I say, sounding weak, no doubt. "I mean, if we don't have to."

To which Tony Passanante replies, cocking his head at me and grinning broadly, "Fuckin' honor is at stake, man."

I don't know. Suddenly, sadly, for no reason that I can explain, I am put in mind of my son, wondering what he would have to say about all this. If I could get him to say anything to me at all about it. I only know that having eaten too much, or drunk too much, probably both, I feel slightly nauseous. I am also vaguely angry with, or sick of, myself. What I really want to do is to get out of there. I've accomplished what I was supposed to accomplish. The two guys are talking to one another again.

"I'll pay the check," I say, and signal to the waitress, who is serving coffee two tables away. She gives me a dirty look that lets me know she'll be over when she has nothing better to do. I stand abruptly, accidentally bumping the table and causing the plateware to clatter. I have out my American Express card, and wave it at the hostess at the front table. She sees me, and comes over in a hurry.

"Everything all right?" she asks.

"Wonderful," I say, "but we're running a little late."

"I'll take it," she says.

"We'll follow you," I say to the woman.

Tony laughs. "Brock doesn't trust her with his gold card," he says to Morrie.

At the front register, Morrie fills his fist with peppermint candies, and Tony lifts a wrapped toothpick, which a moment later he inserts over his lower lip.

"Thanks for the lunch, Brock," Tony says.

"Yeah, thanks, Bill," Morrie says. They both know I will stick Frank with the lunch as a business expense.

"You're welcome," I say, feeling increasingly uncomfortable as we wait for the elevator to arrive at the tenth floor.

As the light goes on, and the door opens, Tony lets escape an enormous belch.

"Leave that outside," Morrie says, and we enter, the two of them laughing, and the doors close behind us.

CHAPTER XII

My father's birthday occurs just four days after my own, each of us having been born under the sign of Virgo, a coincidental bit of trivia to which I attach absolutely no signifigance whatsoever.

My father is 78 today, and we all, including Number One recreant grandson, are on our way to visit him in Massachusetts, where he lives in a comfortable four-room apartment in a four-apartment building that he owns. My father bought the building, and moved into the apartment after my mother died ten years ago. It is understood that we always visit my father on his birthday.

In many ways my father is a remarkable man. He not only manages to take care of himself, cooking his own meals and keeping his apartment neat as a pin, he performs the additional duties of superintending the premises for his tenants. He arranges to have the lawn mowed in summer and the paths shoveled in winter, and if no one shows up to do either job, he does the work himself. He keeps the building in immaculate shape, contracting to have it painted, inside and out, every few years, and recently he had new asphalt shingles put on the roof. He shops for groceries at a nearby supermarket, negotiating his way there and back somewhat precariously in a silver and blue Buick LeSabre.

Nor does he lack for companionship. He is enviably gregarious, with everyone, much more so than I am. A number of regulars drop by to visit my father several times a week, and it says something about him that they are all about twenty years younger than he is (those of his own generation either having died or been shunted away somewhere into nursing home oblivion), and this younger group seems to enjoy the visits with my father as much as he does. His pals (for that is what they are) drop by usually after working hours, the routine being for him to pour them and himself a couple of stiff highballs, and they sit around and chew the fat, as my father says. As often as not on the occasion of these visits, my father will shuffle out to the kitchen and cook up something for them all to eat, everyone seating themselves around the kitchen table. On Saturdays, they sometimes go trout fishing together on a stream that runs through property owned by a private limited member hunting and fishing club that my father has been a charter member of for 50 years. My father's concession to old age is that if they plan to get back after dark, he rides with one of the other members, as the lights of oncoming cars at night interfere with his vision.

My father has a lady friend, Tillie, and although the relationship is exclusively companionable, rather than sexual (a point of insistence he makes to me privately), the feeling between the two is nonetheless close. Merely to hear the name Tillie is to be transported back in memory to childhood Sunday mornings on the floor with the funny papers and the weekly exploits of Tillie the Toiler and her boyfriend, Mac. (Later there were crude booklets circulated among us adolescent boys

136

that had glamorous Tillie copulating next to the filing cabinets with little Mac, his penis the size of a Kosher salami.) I feel certain that if Tillie the Toiler were alive and well, she would look, in her advanced years, exactly the way Tillie Kavanaugh, my father's lady friend, looks today. Tillie is 70, a widow, once pretty, now, perhaps in an attempt to compensate for her age, tending to apply too much rouge to her cheeks and crimson lipstick to her lips. She retired a few years ago from her job in the bookkeeping department of a local department store. She lives in one of the second-story apartments owned by my father, so they see each other every day, often eating supper together in his place (when the guys aren't around), then watching a little TV together before Tillie retires to the privacy of her own place upstairs. She had a mild stroke a year ago that seems to have left no ill effects, but she takes pills to thin her blood, and she has cut back to one whiskey and ginger ale per day.

On the way up in the Pontiac to visit my father, the autumnal change to the north is more advanced, the trees along the highway providing a spectacular display of red, orange and yellow foliage. Beyond the sere meadows and harvested cornfields the distant Berkshire mountains are tinged pink and purple. Some years the foliage is more spectacular than in others, and it seems to me now that this is one of the more spectacular years.

"Look at that!" I call out, and point, as we approach and pass under a particularly brilliant burst of red and orange maple tree foliage. "It's like fireworks!"

"Yeah, Dad, like fireworks," my daughter says. Annie and she giggle, and I presume I am supposed to feel foolish.

"I don't care, it is!"

"Like fireworks!" my daughter repeats, mimicking. And, again, she and my wife are filled with hilarity.

"I'm talking about the burst of colors, it almost splashes out and falls away from the center. You know, I don't mean like fire *crackers*. I mean like *skyrockets*. No, those things that explode in the sky, and cascade down in showers."

"Sure, Dad."

Oh, they're having fun. And, I must say, it tickles me to see them giggling and teasing. I am cruising along at about 65, my new fuzz buster installed and ready to give warning.

"You guys don't see it, do you?" I go on, milking it further.

"Like fireworks!" my daughter repeats herself, exploding again with laughter, like a firecracker herself.

I look in the mirror to see if my son is getting some amusement out of this teasing at the old man's expense. If he is, he is not letting on. He appears to be asleep in the back of the station wagon, and I don't think he's pretending. He was late getting up out of bed this morning, leading me to suspect he may have sneaked out of his room last night to party with his friends.

Actually, it occurred to me last night that possibly he might not be in his room, but I made the mistake of letting my suspicions be known to my wife.

"Of course he's in his room," Annie had insisted. "Your problem is you don't trust him."

"Excuse me," I found myself replying. "Excuse me, but we have a little bit of a track record, I think, in which he has not been altogether trustworthy, wouldn't you say?" This in my snotty British accent tone.

"Then, go out and look in on him," she said.

"I don't want him to think I'm spying."

"Then, if you're not going to do anything about it, stop worrying me about it."

I could strangle her when she's as logical as that. So I didn't go out, but the more I think about it now, I am convinced that he did sneak out last night, and maybe to go off with the Grand Union gang, too.

What is as upsetting to me as anything else is that Annie, I don't think, understands the seriousness of the situation. She wants to believe that there is nothing unusual about our son's behavior. She insists on believing that he is still the nice little kid he always was. Maybe he is. And maybe he isn't. My wife doesn't seem to be aware that the world has changed a lot since we were little kids (on the floor with the funny papers). She doesn't seem to understand that there is some kind of new sickness abroad in the world today, particularly a sickness among the kids coming up. I am absolutely convinced that it is much more widespread, and more serious, than she is willing to acknowledge. And I think it's spreading. How else to explain this sullen, irresponsible, possibly even outright disobedient behavior occurring in our son? It seems to be like an infection carried on the wind, even like a cancer, with a very lethal potential. This nice little kid, crapped out in the back, just happens to represent the future of civilization, in case anybody wants to know, and it doesn't seem to me to be out of line to worry a little bit about the direction he is going in. Frankly, I don't think my son was in his room most of the night, and nobody but myself seems to see the danger inherent in that.

But there is no point in having a row about it, especially

about something you can't prove, anyway. Next time I simply won't listen so much to what my wife has to say, but rather, follow my own suspicions and inclinations.

But now, mulling these matters over, I am aware of a crimp in my chest, a form of discomfort I have been experiencing increasingly of late, and I slip into my mouth a couple of Tums from a small roll I have been trying to remember to carry with me in my pocket for just such times. Which, I think, right there says something, either about me, or about the world. Maybe about both. In any event, the trip that I was enjoying so much up to a few moments ago now, thinking about these things, is spoiled for me, the sense of the beauty of the day now dissipated, the fun of family teasing gone. I hunker grudgingly over the steering wheel, and in my dark mood, in an unworthy effort perhaps to shift over some of my distress onto my wife, I drive faster than I should.

Since Annie says nothing, possibly because she can't imagine what suddenly has come over me, and since her being silent in the face of my irritability oppresses me more than if she were to confront me, I turn on the radio. The airwaves are filled with more news of the hostage situation in Central America. There seems to be no progress, and our government is now reported to be moving two aircraft carriers into the Carribbean.

"They're kidding," Annie says, all of a sudden speaking up, expressing indignation.

"They're not kidding," I say. "Why do you say that?"

"Because the kidnappers will retaliate and kill the hostages."

"That's not necessarily true."

"Well, there's a good chance," she says.

It occurs to me that I might have expected her to take a soft position in this circumstance. Even though my better judgment tells me she is probably right. "Well, they have to do something," I say.

"Yes, they could do something about whatever it is that's behind all this business."

"And you know what that is?"

"It's not my job to know."

"Well, there are a lot of people whose job it is to know who can't get a handle on this thing, honey." A little bit of the British snottiness again. "And I'm sure if there was a chance of doing anything, they would have done it by now." Which, in truth, I don't know whether I believe or not.

"Their idea of doing something is to send in the bombers."

"It is *not*," I say, my irritability clearly revealing itself now. "Maybe there's no alternative. We can't let them run all over us." Perhaps because I feel I have maneuvered myself into a position that I have no idea how to defend, I say this in a very loud voice, and probably in an unpleasant tone of voice, too. It has the effect, anyway, of rousing the prodigal son.

"Could you keep the noise down, please?" he pipes up.

"No! We're having a discussion here!" I shoot back at him. "Maybe you could take an interest in what's going on."

"It's boring."

"It's not boring! *You're* boring!"

"Bill!" my wife interjects.

"What?" Is she about to take his side again? "It's not rock and roll, and it's not dope, so maybe it's too much to expect that he'd care anything about it."

"That's not fair," Annie says.

"Yes. It's fair." I try to catch my son's eye in the rearview mirror. "Our government is about to launch an air strike against guerrilla bases in Central America," I bellow at him. "That's *guerrilla*—terrorists—underground fighters—spelled G, U, E, guerilla, not the kind that swings from trees—"

"Oh, really!" my wife says.

"Yeah, really," my son adds.

"What do you *think* about that?" I ask him. "Is it a good idea, or not?"

"I dunno," he says.

"Well, let me tell you something," I say, glancing over at Annie to catch her reaction. "It may be the only course we have left! Does anybody want to disagree with that?"

"What's the point of disagreeing with you?" my wife says. "You've already made up your mind."

"I have *not* made up my mind! I might not even agree with that position." And sounding truly foolish, even to myself now, I add, hoping to justify the statement I have just made, "But, I have to admit, I'm just a little bit sick and tired of seeing this nation—*us*—being pushed all over the goddamn map by a bunch of—greaseball, dirty, unshaven—"

"Oh, come on!" my wife exclaims.

"—troublemaking—*shitheads!*"

I finish on that note, and there is silence in the car, the others having become momentarily intimidated. I recognize that I have to slide down a bit from the summit of this angry outburst which probably has gone a bit further, a *lot* further, than I had intended it to. "There is such a thing as standing up to bullying," I say somewhat more quietly, hoping maybe that will make some sense.

"There is such a thing as cutting off your own nose to spite your face, too," Annie puts in slyly.

"You haven't answered my question!" I shoot back at her.

"Can we change the subject?" my daughter interjects.

"You want to talk about *shopping?*" I reply, in a manner close to a sneer. I have not come off well in this.

"You stink," she says.

"Wait a minute! Wait a minute! What?" I apply my foot to the brake with such force that the car fishtails, slithering out of control for a moment, until I let up, and it straightens itself out, and we slow down and come to a bumpy and jolting stop on the gravel shoulder of the highway.

"I will not permit—"

"You started it," my daughter says.

"Quiet!" I bellow at her, but now that we are stopped, I really don't know what I will do next. My daughter was the last person I had expected to jump in at me.

"Everybody stop it," my wife says. "If you don't stop it, I'm getting out. I'm not going another mile in this kind of hideous situation."

Nobody says anything. Other cars are whizzing by and blaring their horns at us. In a very quiet, measured tone I say, "It's bad enough what's going on with this kidnapping business. We can agree or disagree about that. I might even agree with what you are saying, although I'm not sure I know what that is. But what really gets to me and drives me crazy, is when children who have been brought up decently and to believe in the decent things of life begin acting in disrespectful ways that are identical—in every respect—to the way these terrorists outlaws are behaving in the news." There. That was what I meant to get at.

Having said that, and with no one immediately coming back at me, I put the car into drive, turning back out onto the highway again. And emboldened, I think by their continuing silence, I turn briefly to my wife for confirmation. "Do you agree?"

My wife looks straight ahead. "I think you're crazy," she says at last.

For just an instant, I realize how close I am to lashing out at her and doing something just terrible. The effort to control the rush of rage within me actually causes my body to shudder, and I grip the wheel even tighter as if to hang on to save my dear life. I have *never* struck at my wife. Nor at my children. Nor, in fact, at any other human being on earth. At least, not since I was twelve years old and got beat up in a fight in the schoolyard over something having to do with marbles.

"We have a difference of opinion on that," I say almost inaudibly, resentfully.

My wife doesn't say another word. Nobody says anything. They are too wise to provoke me further, and we continue along now for the rest of the journey in uninterrupted misery and silence.

CHAPTER XIII

As we turn into the driveway of my father's apartment house, I catch a glimpse of him peering out through his living room window from behind a curtain where he has stationed himself awaiting our arrival. A moment later, as we unload ourselves from the Pontiac, he is at the front door, like a minister at the entrance to his church, grinning and waiting to greet us.

"Well, well, well," he says, jovially greeting the first to approach him, my wife, with a peck on the cheek. My wife and I are not sure, but we suspect he greets her invariably in this same way, neither actually saying hello nor speaking her name, because he has trouble remembering what her name is. This is not because of his age, we have decided, but rather out of long habit. Although over these many years my father has come to have a high regard for my wife, primarily because of her many solicitous attentions on his behalf, there nevertheless is a carryover from the early days when it was in his head that her manner and style, in keeping with the tag end of the radical '60s, were not precisely in accord with what he had envisioned as being appropriate for his son. When I first introduced this new girl with the long hair and granny glasses to my father (more than twenty years ago), he made it very clear that he flatly did not approve of her. During the whole time of our first visit he refused to so much as glance in her direction. Before we left I advised my mother that I didn't care if he liked this new girl or not, but if he couldn't, at the least, be polite, then we would not be able to come up any more. After that, my father always managed to be civil, if not quite polite, but for many years afterward, even long after we were married and my wife gave up her granny glasses for soft contact lenses, it was with the greatest effort that he was able to bring himself to look directly at her and speak her name.

"Hello, honey." This next to my daughter, with another peck on the cheek. We are not sure whether or not he remembers his granddaughter's name, either. We suspect his invariable failure to address her by name is simply an unconscious expression of his disappointment in her for having been born a girl instead of a boy.

"Ah ha! Look at Old Pete! He's grown another foot!" My father is beside himself with glee, as the one and only and latest in the male Brock line, the one to confirm the greatest of all expectations, shuffles up to him, hair in his eyes, eyes averted to the ground, sneakers untied, tie-dyed T-shirt mostly concealed under the blue button-down Oxford Shirt that we have forced him to put on. "You trying to make us all look like midgets, Pete?"

Peter squeezes out a painful smile. He is still growing, but already is about the same height as my father, who is about 5'6". In his prime my father attained a height of perhaps 5'8", but now, at age 78, under the weight of an every-spreading girth, his body has compacted a bit, giving him the appearance not altogether unlike Humpty Dumpty.

And last, to the prodigal son, me, "Hello, there, hot stuff." And craning his neck around for a glance toward the driveway,

"Car looks good." He has noticed, as I suppose I had hoped he would, the result of our having stopped just outside of town to run the wagon through a car wash (with hot wax).

I shake hands with my father, and also give him a peck on the cheek, in so doing noting the familiar sweet cloying spicy fragrance of his after-shave cologne. He is nattily dressed, as always, for which I admire him, though there was a time when I used to scoff at the way he dressed, when he and my mother would come up to visit me at Amherst in their gray flannels and tweeds, and I would meet them in my baggy suntan Chinos and sweater worn out at the elbows, which was *de rigeur* at Amherst at that time. My parents were always horrified, of course, by my appearance, something I have to remind myself of whenever I am startled by my son in one of his death's head T-shirts. It is an irony not lost on me that, in fact, I am wearing today the identical uniform that my father has always worn.

His eyes go up and down over me, from my shoes to the top of my head before a tight smile forms on his mouth and he revolves his body jerkily in a semi-circle and leads the way into his apartment. We follow behind, bearing gifts.

Tillie is standing in the middle of the living room as we enter. We all embrace, and Tillie has a specially warm squeeze for Laura, which my wife and I appreciate as much as Laura does.

"Sit down, sit down," my father says, and as we settle ourselves into the old over-sized easy chairs that I remember from childhood as fitting in better in another larger house, we find ourselves arranged in front of a 24-inch color television set with the sound off but with the picture tuned to a show in which the camera focuses on four females of varying ages, all

147

seated behind a conference table facing a giant wheel spun by a sort of carnival barker in a business suit.

"Make everybody a drink, Bill," my father says. "You know where the stuff is."

I do know where the stuff is, the stuff being a bottle of Seagram's Seven, which I don't really like, nor does my wife. But we will both drink it now. The kids will each have a Coke. Tillie will nurse the drink she already has, and my father, without saying anything, hands me his highball glass with the melted ice cubes, which I take with me out to the kitchen for a refill.

This is an unvarying routine each time we come up. While I am out in the kitchen, I can hear my father saying, "Old Pete, how's the Old Pete?" And when my son croaks out an "Okay, I guess," my father explodes into laughter, seemingly deriving the same kind of enjoyment from this predictable exchange with his grandson as he might from an intricate mechanical toy, say, one of those monkeys with the cymbals and drums that you wind up and set on a table to perform its jerky banging and clanging motions until the spring runs down and you have to wind it up again.

In the living room with our drinks, with the TV still on and the sound still off, my father removes his attention from Pete for a minute, and turns to me. "How's the job going, Bill?"

"Pretty good, Dad. Can't complain."

"You've been traveling, haven't you?"

"I was in Vegas last week."

"Las Vegas? You were? That's where they have all the big shows. Wayne Newton has a big show there."

"Yes, he does."

148

"Your company must think a lot of you, sending you out there."

"Oh, they do," I say.

"Flying out all over the country. That's what the company presidents do. Fly all the time."

I look over at Annie. "I could do without it, Dad."

"Oh, you don't mean that. Flying around the country. That's big stuff."

Why is that I won't gratify him? It would be a simple enough thing to go along with him. Before I can reply, my wife interjects, with a smile directed at my father. "You're right, Grampy. It's big stuff."

My father is not quite ready to let the subject go completely. "It took you a little while," he says, "but you finally came around."

Wisely, my wife, with a quick wink in my direction, jumps in quickly, signalling everyone to gather around the coffee table where we have deposited our pile of birthday gifts.

"Come on, Grampy. Time to open your presents," she says.

"You shouldn't do that," my father says.

"We *want* to," my wife says.

"It's more blessed to give than to receive," Tillie puts in.

Nobody is quick to respond to this. Finally, it is my daughter who says, "That's right. It is."

"Now, what could this be?" My father, with a twinkle in his eye that lets us know he has a pretty good idea, attacks the gay birthday wrapping paper on a flat box that could only hold a shirt or a sweater. "A sweater, I'll bet." And removing the cover and spreading the tissue paper aside, triumphantly he removes a tan wool cardigan.

"How about that?" he says, turning to my wife. "This from you, honeybug?"

My wife, pleased, smiles at him, and nods.

"Good," he says. "My old one was getting a hole in the sleeve."

"I'm glad you like it, Grampy," my wife says, and she gets up, and goes over to him, and gives him a little peck on the lips.

Next is a bottle of his favorite Seagram's Seven, from me, in an oblong box with a plastic bow on the top, which he opens, again with a twinkling in his eyes. "A pair of slippers, I'll bet," he says, sliding out the bottle, and holding it up like a trophy.

"Good boy," he says to me. "This I'll put aside for the gang when they come over."

My wife hands him a little package wrapped by my daughter, which he takes, saying, "What's this? Something from Old Pete?"

"It's from Laura," my wife says.

"Oh?" he says, as though surprised. He claws at the birthday wrapping paper, finally getting it off, and removing a bright yellow ceramic coffee mug which my daughter made for him in school during the last spring term. On one side of it his name is spelled out in different colored glazed letters, as cheerful as a bouquet of flowers. Exhibiting it to the room, but without actually looking at it, or without looking at his granddaughter, either, he says, "Well, well, well."

With a sudden surprising edge in my voice, I say, "Do you know what it is?"

My father clearly does not like being questioned in this manner, because he snaps back at me, "Of course I know what it is." He brings the cup down before his eyes, and says, "A cup."

"It has your name on it," I say. "Laura made it for you."

"Oh?" he says. He rotates the cup clumsily in his hands until he is able to make out the name. "I didn't see that," he says.

"I didn't think you did," I say.

He looks over at my daughter now, perhaps for the first time since she has arrived. "Thank you very much, Sweetie," he says.

My daughter pops out of her chair, and goes over to him and flings her arms around his neck, and gives him a kiss.

"Very nice," he says. And reaches out for the last package on the table which contains, it will come as a surprise to no one in the room, a bottle of his favorite cologne. Before opening it, he gives it a small shake, the twinkle in his eye returning, as he looks over at my son. "This is from Old Pete," he says.

Old Pete shifts uncomfortably, and looks away as my father rips off the paper that my wife has wrapped it in, and holds up high the bottle of cologne. "Ah ha!" he exclaims. "You even know the kind I use." (Which is almost true; my wife knows). My father unscrews the cap, and slaps a generous amount of the cologne on his face, thereby adding a fresh infusion of its spicy scent to the room.

"Thank you, Old Pete!" My father looks fondly over at my son, perhaps hoping that Peter will leap out of his chair and come over to give him an embrace. Pete, instead, extends an index finger, and waggles it at my father, suggesting the offhand manner of Clint Eastwood.

"Well, that was very nice," my father says at last. "Have we got time for another drink?"

We all do take time for another drink, including Tillie, who takes a second "very light" whiskey and ginger ale, and twenty minutes later we are ready to go out for my father's birthday dinner.

My father has chosen the restaurant where we are to take him and has made the reservation himself. We have been here before, to the Coach House. It is a successful enterprise operated by an accountant, one Teddy, and his wife, Marie, who started with a diner ("Good food at an honest price") and not long afterward expanded the premises out half an acre behind the original building. With the opening of the new facility, they introduced a new menu featuring "Continental Cuisine," including such items as veal Orloff and Tournedos Rossini (pronounced "Tornadoes" by the high school girl who is our waitress and who recommends it a few moments later). A four-page raised velvet menu 24″ × 18″ (with a tassle) now lists complete dinners and à la carte "Continental Favorites," together with a list of liquor, beer and wines on the back page. A little card on the table reads, "May we suggest a bottle of Mateus Rosé for your dining pleasure."

The original diner structure remains, but is used now as a ceremonial entryway and reception area, new skylights giving it the appearance of a greenhouse, filled with hanging baskets of plastic plants which we pass under and through on our way to the business end of the restaurant with its Colonial decor of roughcut barnboard siding (no windows) and little coach lights along the walls, illuminating pots of indeterminate plastic red blossoms. The food here is neither good nor bad, but it is plentiful, and to the local folks who continue to come back regularly it is reassuring to know that Marie in her green and black print silk dress and high heels and cradling a stack of menus, and Teddy in his chocolate brown double-breasted suit and orange shoes are still taking responsibility for providing "good food at an honest price."

"Hello! My name is Cindy, and I'm your waitress today. Can I get you something to drink?" The local high school girl appears at our table in mobcap and a Colonial print gown that doesn't quite cover the tips of her blue jogging shoes, sing-songing her announcement, and bringing a pencil up to her order pad.

"That's a good idea," my father says. He has had at least three doubles already, so he is feeling pretty jovial. Actually, the two I have had have loosened me up, too, and I am ready for a third. My wife and I both order martinis, which is what we have wanted all along, anyway. The kids have Cokes, and Tillie has a plain ginger ale.

The drinks come, and ignoring Cindy's recommendations, we all order dinner, my father, the birthday boy, going for the prime rib which will come with bone in, an inch and a half thick and hanging over the edges of the plate. Tillie orders roast Vermont turkey. So does my daughter. My wife will have roast veal, and I will try the lobster tips in sherry wine sauce. My son decides on none of the above, picking, instead, a variety of hors d'oeuvres, including a shrimp cocktail, clams Casino, stuffed mushrooms, and melon and prosciutto, a selection I wish immediately that I had chosen, but which causes ripples of alarm to form on the low brow of Cindy, who will require assistance from Marie on how to bill it. My father doesn't know quite precisely what is going on, but figures it is okay, because it has to do with Old Pete.

The food comes, in gross proportions, and as expected, is

edible, if not exactly exquisitely appealing. But with the effect of the cocktails racing through our bloodstreams, we shovel it in like trenchermen.

It is after we have finished, and Cindy is in process of clearing the table, when suddenly I feel Annie's hand grip my forearm tightly. I turn to her, but she is not looking at me, as I might have expected, rather, she is turned to Tillie who is sitting on the other side of her. Tillie is smiling, which is customary with her, but the smile has something about it of a rigor-like grimace. And I am immediately aware that her head seems to be wobbling slightly on her neck, almost puppet-like. My wife darts a frightened glance back at me. In another instant, Tillie is making little chuckling noises, and a bit of foam bubbles out at the corners of her mouth. My wife springs up, knocking over her chair, and in another instant I am at Tillie's side just in time to catch her from falling off her chair. She cannot possibly be drunk. She is having some kind of seizure.

"Call 911!" I blurt out to Peter.

"What?" he says.

"Tell the manager to get an ambulance!"

Tillie is sitting in the chair, her head tilted sideways as though listening to something attentively, with a kind of leer on her face now, and making little noises that don't quite form into words. She partially raises an arm and gestures vaguely. "Do you want to go to the ladies' room?" my wife asks.

"What's the matter?" my father asks, possibly with a note of irritation. We have interrupted something he was telling Old Pete about fly fishing.

"We're taking Tillie to the ladies' room," I say hurriedly.

My wife and I get on either side of Tillie, and holding her

under the arms we conduct her to the ladies' room, where we
assist her to lie down on a couch. A woman emerging from one
of the stalls is not overly pleased to see me in there.

"She may be having a stroke," my wife says. She turns to
Tillie. "Are you all right, Tillie?"

Tillie moves her head from side to side, then raises it up and
down, producing a combined effect of yes and no that tells us
nothing.

As other ladies are entering the powder room, I go outside.
My daughter is sitting next to my father, and talking to him
earnestly as he sits upright with a worried expression and
fingers the silverware on the table.

"What's the matter with her?" my father asks, as I join
them.

"I don't know. Something's wrong."

"She'll be all right," he says. "She probably ate too fast."

My son joins us. "They're sending an ambulance," he says.

My father frowns. "She'll be all right." He turns to my son,
"Don't be upset, Old Pete."

I get up, and go over to Marie, to follow up on the
ambulance.

"They'll be here any minute," she says. "Is she all right?"

I have no idea whether she is all right. Actually, I am fearful
that she may be dying. I have never seen anybody die, but I
would think this might be the way it would be.

Back at the table my father is talking to the children now,
about how he is thinking of buying a new Buick. Mercifully, it
seems to me, I hear the wail of an ambulance, which comes
closer and arrives outside the building, with a screech of tires
on gravel, which we can hear even through the wall. People at
other tables sense that something has happened, and they are

looking over at us, and at the emergency Exit Door which happens to be located right next to our table.

I am up, and push the bar down, and the door opens, and two hospital medics in white and with a stretcher chair are already about to enter.

"This way," I say, and I lead them to the ladies' room.

"What's the trouble?" says one of the medics.

"I don't know," I say. A moment later they are conferring with my wife, and bending over Tillie who continues to leer and stare blankly.

The medics hoist Tillie onto the stretcher chair, and quickly roll her out into the main dining room toward the exit door near our table. My wife remains behind, while I join the entourage. As we pass our table, Tillie seems to struggle to raise herself from the stretcher, succeeding only in reaching a limp hand out in the direction of my father, who at the moment is stuffing into his mouth a large buttered popover that somehow has been overlooked.

"Hello, there," my father says, as though speaking to a vague acquaintance at a neighboring table. Incredibly, he refuses to look at Tillie, continuing to stare straight ahead as the medics wheel her quickly by, and a small groan escapes from her throat.

"Dad! She's signalling to you!" I hiss at him.

"That's okay," he says. "Hi! Okay." He still doesn't turn, and Tillie is lifted quickly out the exit door.

They slide her into the back of the ambulance, and are about to slam the doors.

"Can I ride back there with her?" I say.

One of them is already in the driver's seat. The other shrugs. "Can if you want."

"I'll just tell the others." But Marie, the owner, has already closed the exit door, and it means going around to the front diner entrance.

"You're wasting valuable time, fella."

There is a moment of terrible indecision. "All right, I'll catch up with you at the hospital."

And the assistant jumps in beside the driver. The lights go on, the hooter commences, and they spin their tires out of the parking area.

I re-enter the building through the front diner greenhouse. At our table the atmosphere is bizarre, with everyone looking bleak and frightened, and my father chatting about the superiority of Buicks over Cadillacs.

"She's on her way to the hospital," I break in.

"Oh?" my father says. "Anything wrong?"

I look at my wife, then back to my father. "They'll find out at the hospital."

"Good," he says. And then adds, "It's too bad. Kind of spoils things for the kids."

Marie, still clutching her menus, approaches my wife and me, and bends over, with a smile in my father's direction, to confer with us privately. It seems they have baked a special birthday cake for my father, and Marie is wondering if they can bring it in now.

"We have a cake, Dad," I say.

"Good," he says. "You think of everything."

Marie smiles, and a moment later, from across the floor of the dining room we have sight of two maidens in Colonial gowns and mobcaps pushing forward a wheeled table with a cake and burning candles, and launching into the first notes of "Happy Birthday to You."

People at other tables immediately join in the singing, and there is nothing for us to do but add our voices, too. My daughter looks horror-stricken. My son mouths the words with neither more nor less enthusiasm than he might while singing his school's anthem, and my father, as always in the past, joins in singing his own praises with gusto, and with a great smile suffused across his face.

"Happy Birthday to Geo-o-o-o-rge," he brays. "Well, well, well," he says after the applause of the entire dining room has died down. "Isn't this nice."

I feel my wife's hand grip mine tightly under the table.

We eat our cake in silence, though my father throws in a few lines of "Old Pete. How's the cake, Old Pete?"

Skipping coffee, shortly thereafter we shuffle out of the Coach House, taking the remaining half of the birthday cake with us in Reynolds Wrap.

"The boys and I will finish this off," my father says.

"Come back again real soon, Mr. Brock!" Marie says to my father.

"We will. Very nice," he says. "Thank you."

I retrieve the Pontiac and drive up to the front of the diner. My wife helps my father into the front seat, and the others climb into the back.

"Very nice," my father says, as we drive off. "Nice birthday."

We drop him and the kids off at his apartment, the kids taking an arm on each side and leading him into the building, while my wife and I remain in the car to go off to the hospital to check on Tillie. My father declines to come with us, giving as an excuse that his presence there would serve no important purpose, and he would prefer to look in on her in a day or two "when she feels better." He says this before we know whether or not she is still alive.

It turns out that Tillie is alive. My wife and I are permitted to visit her in a cubicle behind a sheet in the hospital emergency room. She has a tube down her nose, for what reason I have no idea, and she is conscious and smiles wanly and takes hold of my wife's hand. The intern on duty says she has had a mild stroke, but there seems to be only the slightest paralysis in her right cheek, and that will probably go away, leaving no serious impairment of her speech.

"Tillie's fine," my wife says to my father when we get back to his apartment. He nods and smiles and says, "She probably ate too fast."

I suddenly find myself feeling that if I don't get away from him I am likely to leap on his chest and start pounding on his head. Quickly, and with as little ceremony as possible, I round up everyone and herd them out the front door, leaving it to their own ingenuity as to how best to call out their good-byes and final happy birthday wishes.

With a curt salute of the horn at my father standing on the front porch waving, we drive off, and immediately I am launched into a tirade against him.

"Unforgivable!" I say. "The unspeakable obtuseness!"

"Well," my wife puts in at a certain point, "it's a pretty tough reality for him to have to face on his 78th birthday."

But I am in no mood for conciliation. For the major part of the trip home I can only rage against him. "He's always been this way, Annie." I cannot bring myself to let it alone. Memories of other similar times, it seems, keep roiling up. "Obtuse."

"He doesn't realize," my wife says. "He wants things to be—a certain way. It's his birthday. Birthdays are supposed to be joyous, with a cake and singing. You're not supposed to have strokes in the middle of it."

"Well, too damn bad!" I almost shout it.

"When I told him Peter had a problem at school, he simply blocked it out. It was as if he hadn't even heard me. He actually said to me, 'Isn't that nice.'"

I can only shake my head in dismay.

"He's a man who believes in a kind of—perfection. It doesn't matter what the reality is. He doesn't want to know about it. He removes it from his mind, obliterates it."

I'm thinking now that when I was a child he was always criticizing me. More quietly, I say, "He always wanted everything to be—to come out—just exactly the way he had it fixed in his mind."

"It's not that he's a bad man."

I grip the wheel tightly, squinting into the twilight that is fast approaching. "He's always ending up doing all these unforgivable things."

We drive along in silence. We are not far from home now, having traveled the distance of 100 miles in record time, it would seem. It is almost dark, with the children in the back asleep, and the headlights picking out the underbrush and trees that grow close up to the edge of the winding country road that leads to our house.

In a little while the driveway to our house appears, and I turn into it and bring the car to an abrupt stop. With the engine off, I hunch over the wheel a moment in the dark. The anger of before, in fact, seems to have actually drained away, leaving in its place a lingering dull ache that weighs now on my chest sorrowfully, rather, like a cold and heavy stone.

Suddenly my daughter is awake, sitting up sharply and looking out. "Are we home?" she asks.

"We're home," my wife says. "Wake up your brother."

CHAPTER XIV

Sunday, my day of rest. A week ago today we drove my son to his school. I have a sense of having done nothing since except stamp out fires.

It's another sunny fall day, (We are beginning to hurt for a bit of rain), a good day for football and for scraping the house. As I hunch over late morning coffee and toast, my son already is up on the ladder working away. I can hear through the blast of "The Grateful Dead" the dull scraping sound of his putty knife. A telltale electrical cord runs from a kitchen plug through the slightly ajar sliding doors to the foot of his ladder and the stereo box I bought for him last Christmas. I am now obliged to debate with myself whether or not to go out and ask him to lower the volume. After five minutes of vacillating, I decide finally to let Chet Dowd go and do the dirty deed, if it is too much for him. Though, now that I think of it, Chet may very well be flying to Las Vegas or Honolulu today, and Jane most likely is busy vacuuming or something, and doesn't even hear it.

That settled, I proceed next to tear apart the *New York Times* for the *Book Review* section. I love the *Book Review* section, and spend hours every Sunday lolling lovingly over its contents. After I have gone through *The New York Times Book Review* I have a feeling of restoration, of becoming whole again, of being up on what is happening in the world, my cherished poetic sensibility nourished by new revelations concerning relationships Freud may or may not have had as a child with a distant cousin, new insights into the etiology of Nazism, the appearance of a highly acclaimed first novel written by an overlooked genius who for the past fifteen years has survived by selling firewood in Alaska. I rarely read any of these books. Not that I wouldn't like to read them, but there just doesn't seem to be time, what with dinner, and wine, and TV, and paying bills in my office/den, and also, these books can cost anywhere from $15 to $35, and at the library there is almost always a waiting list of people ahead of me for the one copy of any new volume available.

Anyway, I love the *Book Review,* and, of course, am always on the alert to see if there is anything new by my old pal Pritchard Bates, though reviews of his books are increasingly hard to find, since for the most part they are relegated now to the back fiction round-up pages.

The *Book Review* is buried in the fold of Part II of the real estate section, and it takes a while to find it. On the front page of the news section much space, of course, is devoted to developments on the hostage situation in Central America. The guerrillas are now demanding an exchange of captives, charging that the government has been torturing rebel prisoners. Several Latin America nations have called for a meeting of the Organization of American States. Our State Department in separate notes to all O.A.S. member nations has let it be known that it will not under any circumstances negotiate with terrorists. A group of Congressmen from the Midwest has organized itself around the issue, and a sizable group of members from both parties is calling for an immediate air strike.

The *Book Review* is a bit tame by comparison with all of this, and also, I am feeling a little uneasy and maybe even a little guilty reading it while my son performs his solitary slave work on the side of the house. There is no more boring and tedious job on earth than scraping peeling paint, which is the reason why in the first place I assigned the job to him, as penance. So I debate with myself now as to whether or not I should go out and help him. On the one hand, I don't want to do it, simply because it is Sunday, my day to take it easy; on the other hand, the poor guy probably needs to know that he has not been completely forgotten in his consignment to purgatory. So, I read only half of the *Book Review*, and finally give it up to straggle outside to the rock concert and to see how things are going.

I bend over, and tune down the stereo box so as to chat with my son, which immediately I realize is a mistake, because he darts a black look at me from his perch on top of the ladder. "Dad! That's my favorite tune!"

"Oh. Sorry. Just wondering how it's going."

"It's all right."

"I'll get another scraper, and give you a hand."

There being no response to this, it robs me of any glow of beneficence.

"You want to turn the volume back up?"

"Oh, sure."

I'm trapped now into helping him, and without getting any credit for it, either; and with the volume of the stereo blasting in my ears, too.

I descend to the cellar, find another rusty scraper in the mess on my workbench (which I must clean up some day), and come back up and attack the railing of the front porch to the accompaniment of "Let's Do It in the Middle of the Road."

About an hour of this is all I can take, so I wander over to the foot of the ladder, and stand there for a minute, wondering how long it will be before he will deign to look down. Since it doesn't appear that he will, in fact, ever look down, I am obliged to lower the volume again, eliciting another black look as I call up to him, "How about a break for lunch?"

He stops his scraping for a minute, as though annoyed, and then a moment later descends without saying anything.

"A little lunch?" I say, trying to catch his eye.

"Okay," he says. Hunger forces him to speak, but not to look at me.

Which is my cue to bend over, and snap off the concert, since we will be eating inside.

The girls (okay, women) are off somewhere. I have a sneaking suspicion they are shopping at one of the nearby malls. So my son and I will be lunching together alone.

He goes into the bathroom to clean up, while I locate some hot dogs in the meat compartment of the fridge, which I put on to fry, at the same time heating in a saucepan some chili from a can, and putting some toast in the toaster. Chili dogs, everybody's favorite.

"You want some chopped onion on yours?" This after he comes out from the john. That will be his job, to chop the onions.

"No, thanks," he says.

Okay, so I put the dogs on the table, and we sit down to eat in mutual silence.

I am wondering why he hates me. I can't figure it out. Have I been too tough on him, assigning to him that tedious task of scraping paint off the house? What does he expect after what happened at school? I could have been a lot tougher on him. I haven't bugged him with a lot of lecturing. We had a pretty good talk, it seemed to me, coming back from his school. Sort of a man to man talk, when he indicated for the first time that he actually has ambitions of his own, a desire to do something in life. Could it have been that he was merely feeding me what he thought I wanted to hear? That thought does cross my mind now. I brush it aside, as unworthy paranoia. Still, he doesn't trust me. He expects the worst from me. And, I suppose, I don't trust him. Distrust on both sides. And no resolution. No détente.

So lunch is no fun. We finish, and he gets up from the table, and instead of the gathering closeness that I had hoped to feel I sense within me a resentment rising. A resentment sufficient to rival his own, particularly when he starts out the kitchen slider, without a word of thanks, and even leaving his dirty dishes at his place.

"Dishes," I say, hating myself.

He stops and looks back at me, as though there is something messy on the floor that has caught his attention. "What?"

"Dishes. We put our own dishes in the dishwasher after we have lunch."

His eyes go to his place at the table, and without another word he goes over and stacks his glass precariously on his plate with the silverware and goes to the dishwasher.

"Better rinse them first," I say. It would be difficult to say now who is more angry with the other. "And, if you don't mind, clear off the rest of the table, too."

"Dad!" he protests.

"I cooked! I'm asking you to do your part!"

He doesn't reply, but retrieves the plate from my place, while I am still sitting there. I am not sure, but I feel that the bump against my chair is not wholly unintentional.

"I am getting sick and tired of this!" I suddenly blurt out at him.

"You asked me to clear the table, I'm clearing the table," he says.

"I'm talking about your attitude! If you don't feel cheerful, or if you have something against me, I can't do anything about that. But, dammit, as long as you're in this house, I expect you to act—civilized."

"Like, how?" he comes back at me. "You want me to thank you for putting me up on that ladder scraping the house all week?"

"Do you want me to pat you on the back, and tell you what a great guy you are for getting kicked out of school after being there for only three days?!" I roar back at him. "What the hell's the matter with you? Can't you see anybody else's point of view but your own?"

"You don't understand anything!" he replies bitterly, and starts toward the door.

"Wait! What don't I understand? What don't I understand?"

"Just let me alone, Dad!"

"Wait a minute! I don't know how to deal with you any more. We can't talk. What's the matter with you?"

"Nothing!" And with that, he turns his back on me, and goes outside.

The emptiness of the room resounds like a gong. How did we get to this point? I am ravaged by a mixture of anger and guilt. And I can't tolerate for the moment the guilt, so I nourish the anger. Where is he now? Has he gone to his room? What do I do if he refuses to work on the house?

Gratefully, a moment later I hear a resumption of the rock concert, and the sound of his scraper against the wooden siding. I am relieved, at the same time feeling some imprecise guilt and sorrow replacing anger. I go back to the *New York Times Book Review,* my eyes poring over the columns, but my mind registering nothing.

Annie and Laura have, indeed, been shopping. They arrive back at the house with arms full of boxes and shopping bags, their cheeks flushed with excitement. I am treated to a fashion show, brief glimpses of bright colors held up in a variety of coquettish poses, but all I can think of is what all this must be costing.

"Just a few things we needed," my wife says, and I am aware of myself nodding at her like a dazed boxer. Who am I to know what they need, and what they don't need?

"Everything all right?" my wife asks, looking at me tentatively.

"Oh, yes," I say. "Fine."

Apparently she's not convinced. "Peter's working on the house."

"Yes, yes."

"We thought we'd go out this afternoon, and get some apples and cider. You want to come?"

"I think I'll stay, thanks. Keep an eye on the workforce. I've got a report I ought to do."

I retire into my den/office. It is the one place where I can absent myself from the cares of the world. I am not going to do a report, nor even read *The New York Times*. I am going to sit in my recliner, my feet up, and waste the rest of the day. It would have been better to go for apples with my wife and daughter, but I have no interest in it.

The day passes. At a certain point I bestir myself to go outside and finish up the leaf raking, lugging the last of the lawn debris to the woods behind Chet's house, fairly sure now that he is on his way to Hawaii or Vegas today and won't know. (It's actually good for the forest floor.) At five o'clock I am finished, and Peter, too, knocks off work for the day. Wife and daughter turn into the driveway with a peck of apples and a jug of cider.

We will have baked apples with roast of pork for Sunday dinner tonight, and treat of treats, my wife will bake her annual apple pie. She voluntarily bakes one apple pie every fall, in exchange for which everyone, mostly meaning me, agrees not ever to ask her to bake anything else during the rest of the year. (Sometimes during the Christmas season, by subterfuge means of considerable heavy sighing and pitiable whimpering and rummaging and fumbling through empty canisters in the kitchen I am able to break her down to baking a batch of Daddy's favorite cookies—Carmelitas and apricot chews.)

Dinner is ready at seven o'clock, at the very moment that Mike Wallace is about to interview a Sultan in his palace. The Sultan is believed to have forty-five wives, (Nobody knows the exact number), and I am hoping maybe we'll catch a glimpse of flesh through the gauze, but my wife instructs my daughter to turn off the TV set.

She is right, of course. This is a family get-together, and to be savored, as there will not be too many more of them as time speeds along and the children move on. So I get up from the table and start pushing buttons on the VCR, hoping to hit the right combination, for a change, so as to record the show on tape. Usually I get it wrong, though, in fact, it won't matter, as I rarely get around to watching programs previously taped, anyway.

It isn't exactly a fun-fest at dinner, though everyone is genuinely appreciative of Annie's cooking, Peter even offering a compliment, nodding his head and mumbling, "Not bad."

My wife and I carry on a conversation about nothing, and I ask my son how his studying is coming along.

"I can't concentrate in the house," he replies. "There's too much going on."

"How come? I'm at work during the day. Your sister's at school. Only Mom is here, and she doesn't do anything but lie in bed and eat chocolates all day."

"All right!" my wife says, wagging a finger at me.

"No, really," I say. "It's quiet here, isn't it?"

"Not today, it isn't."

"You've been scraping all day."

"Yeah, but you're going to make me study tonight."

Ah ha! I should have known there was a point to all this. "If you were at school, they have study hall Sunday night," I say.

He knows I've got him on that one.

My wife, the great compromiser, puts in. "Just work for two hours tonight," she says. "You can work in your room, if it's easier for you." She looks at me for confirmation.

"That's okay," I say. "Just make sure you get done what you have to get done. No music."

"Dad," my daughter pipes up in Peter's defense, "music

helps to study."

"It never helped me."

"Because you were listening to that Guy Lombardo dude," my son says, forgetting for a moment and almost allowing himself a small grin.

"It wasn't Guy Lombardo! I never listened to Guy Lombardo."

"Well, the Beach Boys, then." And the grin now simply cannot be suppressed. Apparently there is among a certain cadre of youth even more massive contempt for the Beach Boys than for Guy Lombardo. And to think there was a time once when I had thought my liberal appreciation of the Beach Boys was something I would share in common some day with my children.

"No music while you're studying," I say. "At least, not while you're home."

"When am I going back?" he asks.

"Wednesday. That's your week." A pause. "How do you feel about it?"

There is another pause, and for a moment I am fearful he may tell us that he doesn't want to go back. He *has* to go back! "Yeah," he says. "Whatever."

"Don't say 'whatever'!" I say. "Please! I mean, for your own sake. It's more than 'whatever.' You know that. Don't you? I mean, if you feel, just 'whatever,' it means you don't care. And caring, really, Pete—really—is what it's all about. Do you see that? We're trying to help you."

He nods. But I'm not sure but what he is doing it just so that I won't go on. We're all looking at him, as he pushes his chair back. "Guess I'll get out to my room, and get to work," he says.

172

My heart leaps up. Is that his answer? Or is it that he just can't stand being around us?

"You haven't had your pie!" my wife says.

"I couldn't eat any more now," he says. "Maybe later." He stands.

I am disappointed. I wanted more from him. "Do you want to be excused?" I say.

"May I be excused?" he says.

"Yes, Peter," my wife says softly.

"Thanks. It was good," he says.

Thank you for that, I think. He starts to gather together his dishes to take them to the dishwasher. Is he learning, or is he merely trying to avoid trouble with me? Which is perhaps the same thing.

"You don't have to do that," my wife says, as I frown and grimace at her, and waggle my hand to signal that she should not discourage what he is doing.

" 'Sokay," he says, and totes his plate and glass over to the dishwasher. A moment later he is out through the kitchen slider.

"He didn't eat any pie," my wife says disappointedly.

"His loss," my daughter says. "Yum. I'm gonna have some."

"Me, too," I say. "The heck with him."

"Dad," my daughter puts in, "I didn't want to say anything in front of Peter, but I need a ride to the movies tonight."

"Movies? Have you done your homework?"

My daughter merely rolls her eyes while my wife jumps in. "Yes, she has," my wife says. "And I told her she could go."

"Who's going?" I ask, not objecting now, but nevertheless, I still want to know.

173

"Oh, Missy. And Bonnie. And a couple of others."

"Boys?"

"No. No boys. What difference does it make?"

"I just like to know, that's all."

"Well, now you know," my daughter says. "Will you give me a ride?"

"Now?"

"No, not now. We're catching the last show."

"Which is at what time?"

"9:15, Dad! Gee!"

"Okay, okay. If your mother says okay, it's okay with me."

"It's okay," my wife says.

"All right," I say. "But you come right home."

"I'll need money," she says.

All in all, it hasn't been a bad day. A minimum of craziness, I think we could say, except for the shouting at lunchtime. My son seems to have reconciled himself to the reality of his situation. My daughter and wife are chattering gaily together over something or other that happened during the afternoon. I retire to my den/office with *The New York Times Book Review.*

Freud is, indeed, in the news again, this time it being established that he was a fraud, an opportunist, and a sexual molester. Hitler, it is averred in a new book published in Bavaria, was impotent. The new brilliant novel this week is by an Australian paraplegic lady who writes holding a pen between her teeth. At nine o'clock I am finished. It occurs to me to check the news to see if we are at war, but feeling replenished from my reading chores, I decide, instead, to nourish the good feeling, and try to win a minor Brownie point by taking out to my son a piece of apple pie with ice cream.

"You're not having another piece of pie?" my wife exclaims,

catching me daubing a fat scoop of ice cream onto a plate next to a pie wedge.

"No, I'm not having another piece of pie," I reply, mimicking her tone. "I'm taking it out to Peter."

"Oh, that's nice," she says.

We have a spotlight attached to the outside garage/studio, but, of course, the bulb is burned out, since no one other than Daddy ever remembers to turn it off when it's not needed. I am making my way gingerly in the dark when out of nowhere all of a sudden I stub hard against the ladder my son earlier in the day must have dropped flat there across the driveway. By executing an incredible leap that Baryshnykov wouldn't have believed possible I am able to save myself from a bad fall. Even more miraculously, while still in the air—and in the dark!—I am able to snag in my left hand the scoop of ice cream that has been propelled forward in a looping trajectory, a fielder's choice that I am proud of but immediately regret. Standing there in the dark with the freezing lump squished between my fingers, I scrape it off onto the plate next to the pie, and lick my palm and fingers before, finally, wiping the back and front of my hand across my shirtfront.

Enthusiasm for the mission somewhat dampened, I nevertheless manage to negotiate successfully the remaining terrain over to the stairway leading to my son's room, and grope my way up, gripping the railing with my free hand, taking care to keep my body away so as not to catch my pants on any nailheads.

When I reach the top landing, as customarily, I immediately start humming loudly, clearing my throat, and stomping my feet, so as to alert my son in case he has temporarily put aside the books in favor of an early evening massage of the upright organ. Light leaks out around the edges of the cardboard stapled across his window and from underneath the door. I don't hear any rock music, so apparently he has obeyed my stricture against listening to the stereo.

I knock softly, anticipating the growl from within that normally greets any such intrusion. (He'll feel guilty when he sees me standing there holding a piece of pie and ice cream for him.)

He doesn't answer. It could be that the delights of Algebra II and the Early History of the American Nation have charmed him to sleep in his chair.

I knock louder. "Peter!" It's possible, too, that it's simply taking him a few minutes to tuck his pecker back out of sight before getting up to let me in. Could he be cheating on me, with the blast of the rock concert piped in through earphones?

"Hey, Pete!" I pound on the door. He ought to be able to hear that. "Wake up, buddy!"

Quiet as a tomb. Which isn't quite right, either, it seems to me. The first fearful intimation that perhaps something is wrong suggests itself. Electrocution by stereo connection, right now the music beating into his dead body through singed ear canals. The slip of a knife while sharpening a pencil to write a school essay! (How would that son of a bitch headmaster like to live with that on his conscience for the rest of his life?) The possibilities proliferate. A depressed state occasioned by rock music deprivation, resulting in a razor slash across the wrist, or a belt around the neck attached to a ceiling spike.

"Pete! Can you hear me?" I'm banging on the door now. If Chet Dowd is home, I'm sure *he* can hear me, and shortly will be extending his head over the hedge. I try my son's door now,

176

rattling it uselessly. Naturally, it is locked, and he is the only one who has a key, a circumstance that you can bet will be corrected tomorrow. I am aware for the first time of a burning sensation in the arch of my foot where I banged it into the ladder, and a feeling of cool stickiness about my instep, blood, I think, having run down inside my shoe. Ignoring that for the moment, I put down the plate of pie and ice cream, and move quickly to the window, which I can see is also locked. Adrenalin is pumping now, and my breathing is coming heavy. Kicking off the shoe of the non-injured foot, I hammer the heel against the glass near the latch, and stick my hand through the broken shards to unlock it. I am able to get it open, and rip back the cardboard, throwing a leg over the sill drawing my body in behind.

Flinging aside the tie-dyed seraglio sheets, I expect the worst, my son lying on the floor, wired body twitching in time to a rock beat, wrists floating in pools of blood.

He is not there.

He has sneaked out. Is it possible he is inside our house, having entered, for who knows what reason, through the front door as I was letting myself out the back? A last straw to grasp at. If it is, indeed, the case, it will be difficult explaining why I broke his window.

I let myself out his door, making sure the lock is left open, and in the dark accidentally manage to boot the pie and ice cream off the landing. I make it to the house without further mishap, minding, of course the ladder in the driveway.

"Hello! Anybody here?!" I sing out, as I come into the kitchen, and find my wife at the kitchen table reading the Sunday *Times*.

"Hi!" Annie pipes up cheerily. "How'd he like the pie?"

"He's not in here?"

"No." The first look of alarm enters my wife's face.

"The little bastard has sneaked out!" I roar. "I had to break his window to get into his room, and he's not there!"

My wife's eyes go over me quickly, focusing a moment later on the blood that has soaked through my sock and is drying on my Chinos.

"You cut your foot," she says, in some alarm.

"That was on the ladder!"

"What were you doing up on the ladder?"

"It doesn't matter! He's not in his room!"

Her eyelids close slowly over her eyes, and she lowers her head in anticipation of the coming storm.

CHAPTER XV

I can't believe this. In deliberate defiance of the rules we have laid out expressly, my son has sneaked off. No. I can't believe it. He is out there, in his room. I simply missed him somehow, he is in hiding there, or sleeping, possibly engrossed in study, ensconced behind a particular sheet, some *trompe l'oeil* scrim of fabric which I failed to look behind in the labyrinth of his den.

Peering out through the kitchen sliders, I can see the lights on in his room. Did I leave them on, or has he returned already? Grabbing a flashlight, I take myself back out to make another check.

At his door, I knock, and call out, and push into the room, all in the same instant, expecting this time, certainly, to find him standing there, most likely scratching his head, and looking at me, like he's supposed to, like a hobo interrupted by his campfire.

He is not there. Of course, he isn't. The fact that I have known really that he wouldn't be doesn't lessen the disappointment. Maybe he has left a note. Or, at least, some kind of evidence. Of what, I have no idea. I poke behind and underneath the ripped black leather sitting chair that he favors, that he slumps down in to hold court when his pals are over. God knows what they do, listen to their music, I guess. My son and I together hauled that chair from the local dump one day, toting it in the back of the station wagon, I have a ripped triangle of fabric in the ceiling of the car to remind me.

I don't see anything that would be of any help. The eternal flame flickers from the candle in his coffee can cover. That's dangerous! Leaving an open flame burning. I pinch the wick, noting as I cool my thumb and finger with a whiff of breath little blackened shavings scattered about the base of it. They look like chars of burnt-out tobacco, droppings from a pipe. Though not tobacco, I have a sneaking suspicion. Something rougher cut. I could kill him. I lick a finger tip and adhere one to it, splicing into it with my front teeth, somewhat surprised not to detect the expected burnt hemp taste. I chew on it a little more vigorously. Perhaps it isn't hemp. There is very little taste at all, actually, perhaps a hint of something salty, a bit sour, with the texture of wax, something like *feces.*

"Shit!" It's a mouse turd. Exclaiming and blowing it out in an explosion of spit across the room. I'm not a connoisseur of mouse turds, but you don't have to be a genius to know that that's what it is. It's a mouse turd, a whole plate full of them. I fling the coffee can top with the affixed candle through the open door, mouse turds flying in every direction about the room.

Furious as I am at having bitten into a mouse turd, I am at the same time relieved, I suppose, that it wasn't a hashish ash. Still, I am in an unforgiving mood. He should have told us, at the least, that there were mice running around his room. What kind of irresponsible, filthy behavior is that, to live in harmony with mice running around your candle? He probably watches them in a hallucinatory state, and thinks he's Cinderella, or somebody. He's been smoking weed down there. I know it. On a heroic high, he has summoned up the courage to defy us, and leave the compound, most likely in a search for more dope.

"He's not there!" I exclaim to my wife, going immediately to the kitchen sink and rubbing ivory liquid onto my front teeth.

"Why are you putting dish-pan soap in your mouth?" my wife asks, irrelevantly, and with a puzzled expression.

"I'm cleaning my teeth," I growl at her. And back to the point, "He's run off!"

"He'll probably be back in a minute. Maybe he ran his bike over to the store for a soda."

"It's Sunday night. The store's closed! He's gone over to the parking lot to score dope!"

"Oh, Bill!" my wife exclaims.

"Don't 'Oh, Bill' me! He's been smoking down in that room. And there are mouse turds all over the place!"

My wife looks at me again with that same puzzled expression. "Mouse turds?"

"I bit into a mouse turd!" I run a paper towel over the front of my teeth, spit a few times into the sink, and take a glass of water. It still seems as though I can taste mouse shit. "I'm going after him."

"Where?"

"I don't know! Wherever he hangs out! The parking lot! The bowling alley! The arcade!" As I reel off the list of places where most likely he might be found, it occurs what a dismal gallery of choices he allows himself. It is that outlaw mentality I have noted, the desire to immerse himself in sheer ugliness, ugliness for the sake of ugliness.

"Why not wait for him?" my wife says. "He'll be back probably before long."

"Yeah, yeah," I find myself jeering at her. "Maybe we should greet him with a reward, a medal when he comes skulking back, thinking we don't know that he's gone."

"We didn't tell him he couldn't go out," my wife says.

"We did! It was explicit. He was to study in his room, without music, without visitors. Is that permission to sneak out and score dope?"

"He's not going after dope!" my wife says, showing impatience with me.

"He is! And even if he isn't, he is acting totally in defiance of the rules we set down for him!"

"He's only fifteen, Bill!" my wife exclaims.

"And about time he learned some respect!" Which I think is absolutely the point of this whole business. And I follow this up with a rigid finger aimed in a direct line with her eyes, to say, "This is it, Annie! We let him get away with this, and it's over! He'll feel he can do anything he wants. We're some kind of joke! He doesn't have to listen to us. He can do whatever the hell he wants. Well, the hell with that! I am not a joke. I am not a joke!" And, whatever her answer is to that, I don't know, because I am on my way out the door, and if I do say so, I feel better, at least for having said what I had to say.

Before I can get into my car, there is an importunate cry from my daughter from the front porch.

"Dad! Are you taking me?"

"What?!"

"To the movies! You promised to drive me to the movie."

"Hurry up!" I call.

"I got to get my jacket."

"Never mind your jacket!"

But she doesn't listen. She's getting like the rest of them. She runs back inside the house. She's probably right, she really needs a jacket, it's getting nippy, but for Christ sake, I've got more important things to take care of now than to chauffeur her to the movies.

She's with me in another moment, smelling strongly of the splash of perfume she must most certainly have dumped on herself when she ran back in to get her jacket. So. There will be boys there.

I back out jerkily, and spin the tires heading up the street.

"Wrong direction, Dad!" my daughter says, somewhat condescendingly. She is getting to sound more like my son every day.

"I know what I'm doing. You're going to have to wait a minute," I tell her. "I got to check out something first."

"I'll be late," she says, and she slumps down into her seat, reaching a left arm forward and flicking on I-95, which around here everybody knows plays the craziest rock music.

"You don't have to have it that loud," I say.

"If you can't hear it, you might as well turn it off," she says.

"I didn't say you couldn't hear it, I asked could you turn it down. Never mind. Leave it up." And by that, I hope to shame her into turning the volume down, but she doesn't fall for it. She accepts what she has been allowed, and the music blares.

Our town is small enough so that there are clearly defined areas where particular groups of kids go to hang out at night. The jocks, of which my son is not one, tend to gather inside and outside on the sidewalk in front of Mario's Pizza Parlor, on Main St. (where they can be seen, at least, if their parents should care to ride by just accidentally, and want to wave at them). On Saturday nights there are dances at the high school, and the jocks usually go there. After the dance, they go to Friendly's and have cheeseburgers and ice cream. (McDonald's and Burger King have been trying to get a franchise in town for years, but every time they apply, there is an outpouring of solid opposition from the community, I am glad to say, the point being that we don't need yellow arches behind the steeple of the Congregational Church.) After they have pigged out on banana splits, they pull into a side lot of Hibeck's all-night Mobil station and variety store, where they sit and smoke cigarettes and listen to milder forms of rock and roll and disco and look to see who else is doing the same thing. I get all this information from my daughter, who has had dates with some of the jocks. She is *au courant* as to what goes on, and as we pass Mario's now, the group is gathering there, and I suppose my daughter has plans to meet some of them later after the movie.

"I want you home right after the flick," I say. "Do you have a ride?"

"We'll get one," she says snippily.

For years she has been my ally, and this new nastiness is still something I am not accustomed to dealing with yet.

The non-jocks hang out mostly in the aforementioned downtown park, summer and winter, rain or shine, at the edge of the Grand Union parking lot; also, as noted, at the bowling alley, mostly in the johns, where they pass around joints, and at the video game arcade, also repairing frequently to the johns. It is a mostly masculine fraternity, though there are no overtones of homosexuality implied, I don't think. Once in a while you will see in their midst a couple of girls looking as raggedy as the boys. Sometimes at night, they will move their campsite into the nearby town woods, and light bonfires, and sit around and tell ghost stories, and smoke weed, and roast squirrels that they catch in homemade snares. All of this in grudging bits and pieces I have gotten from my son, who in a different area is as *au courant* as my daughter.

Parked near their parking lot enclave there is usually a truck or two, a beat-up old Ford LTD, and a couple of street motorcycles. Every so often one of the gang will mount a motorcycle and with an ear-splitting roar do a racetrack run on one rear wheel in front of the supermarket entrance, usually managing to terrorize some old lady with a weak heart trying to get from her car to the store without falling down. There have been letters of complaint to the weekly newspaper on this.

At night, they are there, too. As some slink away to eat or defecate or rob houses or stab their parents or do whatever else they do besides stand in the parking lot, others come to take their places, the glow of their cigarettes in the dark flaring and making little arcing movements as they shuffle about, doing nothing, waiting. If you think much about them, as I do, at least I do whenever I go to the supermarket and catch sight of them, their constant presence in the parking lot is a torment, whether because of Peter's attraction to them, or simply because of their disfigurement of the landscape, or both. And I am convinced they know precisely the kind of terrorizing effect they have upon us all, and I wonder if that has not become their single most important purpose in life at this time, to make the lives of the rest of us a little big uglier, like their own.

Although it is illegal, on warm summer nights some of them sleep out in the park under bushes. If you should walk through the park on any morning, the detritus of their night's bedding down is all about, beer cans under bushes, cigarette butts on the gravel paths, empty corn chips bags and yogurt

185

containers crumpled up. I am reminded that it is about time that I wrote a letter to the editor of *The Courier* on this.

Even on rainy days, they are stationed there. Going to the store, you look over in the direction of the park, and there they are, shoulders hunched under the dripping trees, wearing a variety of floppy hats and dirty bandanas on their heads, smoking whatever they are smoking, and peering out at the world, looking cold and bitter and wizened, like Andean peasants waiting for a day's ration of coca leaves.

We have persisted in believing that our son is different from the others, that despite his attraction to them, he has not yet become hardened into the same disaffected mold as the others. On my way to the parking lot now in the Pontiac, with my daughter, the thought crosses my mind that we may have been wrong. My son has pulled back from his school, deliberately gotten himself suspended so that he can be sucked up again into their midst, hardened perhaps by this experience. Harder now than before. It's possible. I hope I'm wrong. We're going to find out, though, and soon. I don't intend to go on indefinitely living with this indecision hanging over us. If, indeed, he is determined to flaunt his independence in our faces, if he wants to challenge us to see how weak we are when he challenges the power, he may get a surprise. Does he think I won't come down on him? I am not going to be one of those fathers who becomes silent and defeated and walks around the house disappointed and at the same time afraid of his own son. Fuck that! I may have to take some crap now and then from Frank at the office, but I don't have to take it from my own kid. We'll see about dignity. I run my house, and I do what I can to make our lives as civilized and sane as possible, and if that's not the way some punk kid who happens to be my son

186

wants to play it, go ahead! Sleep under a fucking bush! Don't come home for a shower, though. Stay away! Get out of my life!

I am thinking these things, and making myself sick, as I almost run into a Pinto in front of me that has stopped short for a light. Jesus! I give that idiot the horn.

Somewhat embarrassed at having my daughter see me in this agitated state, I look over at her for a reaction. She is looking straight ahead, and snapping hard on a wad of gum she has slipped into her mouth. Without offering anybody else any, of course.

I pull into the Grand Union parking lot, which is mostly empty because it is Sunday night. I glance over to the edge, toward the park. There they are, the gang, waiting, watching.

"What are you going to do?" my daughter asks, a note of dismay in her voice. She turns off the radio.

"I'm going over and have a talk with some of those guys."

"Oh, Dad, give it a rest, will you?"

"What do you mean, give it a rest?"

She turns away, and looks straight ahead, snapping her gum. "Never mind," she says.

"I'm going to talk to those guys!"

"Fine," she says. And she slumps down in the seat so that looking into the car from outside you would never know anyone was in there.

There is no reasoning with her, at least not now. I plan to have a few words with her later, though. She is definitely getting out of line, in my opinion.

I get out of the car, and head over in the direction of the gang, keeping a dignified bearing about me, taking my time.

They are bunched together, about ten of them. They make

no move to part as I approach and edge my way carefully into their midst. The feeling I have is a little bit like it might be were I to wander into a terrorist enclave. They look me over, very little expression on their faces. I am not afraid, actually. I know they won't bother me, not in these circumstances, in the center of town. It might be different if I were to stumble across them sitting about one of their bonfires in the nearby woods, roasting a squirrel and smoking dope. It is not clear what this roasting of squirrels is all about, but my son has indicated they catch these animals, and roast them over fires, and eat the meat. Squirrel is all right, something like rabbit, though tougher, but I'll bet these guys are not eating squirrel for the delight of it, or even because they are hungry. (They always seem to have enough money to buy corn chips and yogurt from the Grand Union.) Their intent has to do more with outlaw ritualism of some kind. At least, that's what I surmise.

I know a couple of them, from past encounters. I have been here before. Their ringleader, one Rasky, is present, standing in the back. Sometimes he is sullen, at other times expansive (depending on what drug he is on, I suppose). Our eyes meet. To me, his eyes look glazed and possibly hypoglycemic. He steps forward, a big grin breaking across his unshaven, stubbly face.

"Mr. Brock! How ya doin', Mr. Brock? Got a cigarette, Mr. Brock?"

Without being able to say precisely why, I know that the repetition of the name somehow is assaultive, having about it a brazenness, arrogance.

"I don't smoke," I say.

"That's okay, Mr. Brock. How about a dollar. Have you got any money?"

188

"Have you seen my son? I'm looking for my son." It occurs to me that I probably have never acted more dignified in my life, and without any phony British accent, either. Just straight dignity. I wonder how Frank would handle this one. Probably he wouldn't be in such a position in the first place. A hurtful thought.

"No. No way. Haven't seen him, Mr. Brock. Not since you sent him away to that reform school."

"It's not a reform school!" I snap at him, raising my voice. Rasky's grin broadens, as he sees he has touched a sensitive nerve. Is this his main pleasure in life, discomfiting others? He's good at it, no doubt of that. Well, he's been practicing. He is a kid of about seventeen, missing a front tooth, with a four-day stubble of beard and blondish somewhat matted hair streaming out from under an Andean hat, down to his shoulders. His father, Peter has told me, has kicked him out of his own house, and it is said that he lives wherever he can find a place, in friends' cars, in the park, on the sidewalk. His family has given up on him, and very likely he is close to being destroyed, on his way to spending a life of little more than harboring grudges against those who have more than he has. I hate him, mostly because I can see the conflict in our own home ending up in the same way.

The worst part is, there is something physically attractive about these kids, I can't help observing it. Well, they're *kids*. It's hard to find an ugly kid. Rasky could be attractive, if he would take care of himself. But, of course, that's the point, he doesn't. He never will. He has given up on the world in which people take care of themselves. For the rest of his life he will dedicate himself to bitterly wasting it, idling about, not believing that there are any opportunities open to him, until

189

boredom itself will trick him into some new kind of assaultive escapade. He will do something criminal. But, like all criminals, he will underestimate the power of the establishment, which suddenly will swoop down on him, the way he swoops down on one of his squirrels, collaring him, putting him in a cage, and when they let him out, if they do let him out, he will know only that the world is truly his enemy, his only remaining ambition to ravage it, rape it, plunder it, terrorize it.

"He tells me it's like a reform school," this creature says.

"You just said you hadn't seen him!" I pounce on the remark.

"Oh." His hand comes to his mouth, not even pretending to hide the impish grin behind it. The others around him all shuffle and look away and grin and hunch their shoulders. One of the younger ones, standing next to his bicycle, hops into the seat, lifts the fork in the air, and rides off on one wheel, rolling outward in a curve, then circling back across in front of us.

"Just for a minute. He came by."

"When?"

"I dunno." He looks around at his confrères. "When was he by? A few minutes ago."

"Where was he headed?"

"You tryin' to catch him, or sumthin', Mr. Brock?"

They all think this is hilarious, and they look at one another, and run their tongues around in their cheeks, and peer off into the black red night glow over the Grand Union.

"Yes, I am," I say. "I want him home. I don't want him hanging around here. I don't want him to have anything to do with you guys." And I look Rasky straight in the eye, wondering what he will say to that. Sometimes there is no other course than the absolute truth.

For just an instant there is a look of pain in his face, I have succeeded in touching some still unprotected area within him, before he says, looking straight back at me, "What've you got against me, Mr. Brock? Did I do something to you?"

"I don't like the way you live, Rasky," I blurt out at him. "I don't want my son to be like you."

He looks back at me, his eyes in little slits now, and he manages to bring something of a harder look into his face. "He's more like me than he is like you," he says.

"That's a lie!" I almost scream at him, my face only a few inches from his dirty stubble now. I am wondering if he will take a poke at me. I would go for his throat if he did. I'd kill him. "Over my dead body, Rasky. Over my dead body!"

We are staring into each other's eyeballs now, neither willing to back down. I have the feeling his stare must be like that of criminals I have read about, who look at you until you turn away either in fear or embarrassment. But it is he who backs down from the criminal gleam in my own eyes. The cruel slit of his mouth seems to spread out into a concessionary smirk, the look of bravado not quite concealing the fact that I have hurt him as much as he has hurt me. It is a standoff.

Without another word, I step around him, and with a certain dignified presence, I think, push through the group standing about, moving toward the blackness of the nearby town park. Let one of them touch me. If Peter's in the park, crouching under a bush, hiding, having seen the Pontiac come into the parking lot and having fled, I'll find him. I'll drag him out, by the ears. He will not be more like Rasky and his crowd than he is like me. I will not stand for it. Over my dead body, will it ever be so. A meaningless cliché phrase, but it sticks in my mind, as I find myself scrambling along the park paths now, veering off and peering under bushes crazily, then coming back on to the paths, panting for breath, but not giving up, exhaustion feeding my frenzy. Over my dead body, will he turn out like those others. My dead body, and his.

It is then that the little kid with the bicycle who rode away a moment ago comes along the path behind me, coasting fast, just barely missing me, and hisses in my ear as he passes. "Asshole," he says.

This little thirteen-year-old, who doesn't even know me, just rode by, almost hitting me, and calls me an asshole. Is this what life has come to in our time, kids gratuitously hurling obscene insults at their elders, their betters?

"Fuck you! You little shit!" I shout after him. And suddenly, I am running, trying to catch him. Though he is on wheels, nevertheless, I think I can catch the little bastard. What I will do if I catch him I have no idea, but I will catch him, and I will grab him by the throat and scare the shit out of him!

At this hour, the gates to the park are all locked, except one, the one we both entered through. Therefore, though I know I cannot catch him on the paths, I can cut across grass once he commits himself to a particular path. He probably is surprised, also a little frightened, I hope, that this old fart is, indeed, coming after him, he not having thought out the consequences of his action in advance, any more than I am thinking out now in advance what I am doing, or why I am doing it.

I simply know that my strategy is to corral him back toward that sole gate that is open to the park, which I intend to hang back from until he commits to it, and then I will race across grass and maybe, just maybe, catch him as he tries to get out. The old-timers sitting on their benches cringe as I lurch past them, seeing something threatening perhaps in my effort. Let them worry, I feel exhilarated in a way, that I can do this, just the kind of thing I did when I was the kid's age that I am chasing. It is behavior long gone that comes back to me as naturally as if I had been in training for it ever since. Fight! Fight! It's as though a fight is shaping up in the schoolyard, and I'm ready!

And then he commits to the gate, and I take off across grass after him. It is going to be close. He is coming down a path along the far fence, and I am going directly at the gate, running in my good shoes, and feeling my damaged instep warm and wet, but not hurting. My only concern is not to stumble now. My momentum is truly surprising, and I am leaning into the run, and the danger is, I know I could easily over-run my own feet, and fall. But I am keeping up with my own legs. It is going to be very close, whether I catch him or not. Though I think I will, and the possibility of success fuels a new burst of speed. I am going to carry this one off.

Then, just when it looks as though I will have him, one of the old couples, oblivious to all except possibly the chill of the evening and their aching bones, stands directly in front of me, I see this old man with a cane and the bent old lady holding onto his arm, and the terror in their eyes as I bear down on them. He starts to the left, to avoid me, but because the old lady's arm inhibits his movement, it is more of a feint than a movement, fortunately, because I, too, have opted for the left, and just miss ploughing into him, even so executing another brilliant Baryshnykov maneuver to avoid knocking them both

193

over. My own agility is a miracle in itself, powered by my pumping muscles. But, meanwhile, the kid on the bike does a park skid at the gate, then accelerates and goes on out through. I scoot around the old couple, but the kid is out now, on hard parking lot pavement, moving away, as I come back through the gate, running through the gang who have parted to let their friend through and stand now, and cheer as I puff by, exhausted.

"How to go, Mr. Brock!"

"Go get 'im, man!"

"Who is that kid?!" I bawl at them, half stopping, but still moving forward. "I want his name!"

"I didn't even see him, Mr. Brock. Did any you guys see anybody?"

The kid is at the far end of the parking lot now, and has stopped, and with one leg slung over the bar of his bike, he looks back, catching his breath.

"Ass-h-o-o-o-o-le!" he croons into the night. And I am aware now only of my pumping heart, a wet shirt, a rising sense of foolishness, the gasping for air, and in the near distance, the head of a little girl rising from behind the dashboard of my Pontiac to see what is going on, then just as quickly slithering back down the seat again out of sight.

"I'll get you! You little shit!" I cry back into the night. "I'll get you!"

Even more than a few moments ago, I feel like I remember feeling once back in sixth grade—even before I went into junior high school—the time another kid and I stood in the playground yard, and hurled insults at one another as a crowd gathered around, urging us to fight, and because we didn't know what else to do, one or the other pushed the heel of his

194

palm against the other's shoulder, which caused a response in kind, and then another response, harder now, and suddenly a push was a punch, and in the next instant we were rolling on the ground, and punching and tearing our clothes, until Miss Keegan, and I remember her well, and remember her name, grabbed both of us, by the ears, and led us off to the principal's office. Both ready to cry, and feeling we had somehow done something terribly demeaning, unworthy and foolish.

And as I drag myself back to the Pontiac, gasping now, wondering if the end result of all this will be a heart attack here in the parking lot, where the only people who could rescue me are standing 75 feet away, with sneers on their faces, I open the car door, and plop myself into the seat.

"God, Dad!" my daughter growls at me from her recumbent position under the dashboard, "What are you *doing?*"

"Wait a minute!" I gasp at her. "Don't start in!"

"Right!" she says. "Are you through playing with the kids?"

"Do you think it's right that a little thirteen-year-old kid should come up to me in the dark on his bicycle, and practically run over me, and call me an asshole?" I have never used the word asshole in front of my daughter before, I don't believe.

"That's not the point," she says, still staying down. "Are you on the same level he is?"

"What was I supposed to do?!" I bellow at her.

"I don't know!" she practically screams at me. "But I'd think you could handle it better than that."

"Sit up in that seat!" I say to her, and I turn the key in the ignition.

My daughter is frightened of my tone, I think. She never has been frightened of me before. My ally. Are we becoming adversaries? Is she turning on me? "Just drive out of the parking lot," she manages to say in an icy tone.

"I said sit up!"

"I don't want anyone to know you're my father," she says.

I could almost belt her. It is my first reaction, to hit my own little daughter, as it recently crossed my mind to strike out at my wife when we were in the car going up to see my father. What is happening to me? I spin the wheels, turn the steering wheel hard, and head out of the parking lot. I am not sure, but above the noise of the vehicle, I think I hear a chorus from behind me, "Ass-h-o-o-o-le!"

I could spin around, and drive directly at them. I'd get one or two of them before they could all scatter to safety. Maybe that kid on the bike, I could catch him.

"Sit up," I say to my daughter again.

She brings her head up to window level, peeks out, and then allows her body to rise to a semi-sitting position.

"I would like to know—" I begin, but I am not to finish. She reaches to the radio, and turns on her I-95 at incredible volume.

"This is my car!" I say. I reach to the radio, and snap it off, then immediately have a better idea, punching it back on, and to 1010 WINS, "You give us 22 minutes, we'll give you the world." And turn the volume as loud as it will go. She wants volume, she'll get volume, *my* volume.

"All the news all the time." Here's an update. It has been reported unauthoritatively that a detachment of Cuban troops has been sighted setting up anti-aircraft gun emplacements in the locale of the terrorist kidnappers. Meanwhile, the terrorists are hanging tough, threatening to cut the throats of the American advisors the minute they hear the sound of approaching planes. Our government is meeting with the families of the hostages, explaining that the sacrifice of these men may be necessary so as to set an example to terrorists world-wide, to let them know that we will not tolerate under any circumstances interference with the rights of U.S. citizens abroad.

"Let me out," my daughter says.

"Do you want to go to the movies, or don't you?" I bellow at her over the news.

"I can walk from here."

"You can go home, too." To strengthen the threat, I look over at her, slowing down and pulling over to the side of the street. I don't want to force her to return home, but she is pushing me. "Is that what you want?" I ask. We are stopped now at the curb, the radio still blaring. "You decide."

My daughter suddenly opens the car door, springs out, and dashes over to a grassy bank nearby, and starts clambering up it.

Again, that adrenalin feeling rushes through me. There is a second when I open my own door, with the idea of going after her.

"Where are you going?" I call after her.

"To the movies!" she shouts back.

I can't go after her. I doubt if I could catch her, anyway. And what would I do, if I caught her. Spank her? Wrestle her back into the car? She'd probably jump out while it was moving. What am I doing? She can't bear to be in the same car with me. I sit there a minute, and watch her frail body disappear over the crest of the bank. I have no choice but to let her go. I have never felt so defeated, so crushed, so hurt, in my entire life. I don't know what to do about it.

I snap the radio off. "Bastards!" I mutter.

I have no choice but to take myself home. Maybe my son will be there, after all this. What keeps coming to mind is the matter of dignity.

I come in the front door at home. I don't see my son lurking about anywhere. At least, he is not in the kitchen in front of the open door of the refrigerator, where I would expect him to be. My wife is on the phone. Why, on the phone? She never talks to anyone on the phone at this hour. I don't catch any of the conversation. She is at the end, saying good-bye, but from the tone of her voice alone, I know her well enough to know that this is a serious call.

She hangs up the receiver, and turns and looks at me.

"Peter's been arrested," she says.

CHAPTER XVI

My life is falling apart.

"What happened?" I am standing over my wife who is seated, her hand still resting on the phone on the kitchen dining table. She looks up at me, as if she has been clubbed, raped.

"He was in the park—"

"I know."

"—and apparently one of the other boys—one of the older ones—went into the Grand Union and bought a six-pack of beer."

"Did Pete tell you this, or the cops? Did you talk to Pete?"

"Yes. Peter told me."

"Did you talk to the cops?"

"Yes." She gives me a look of annoyance, an indication she would like me to understand she is capable of relating what happened without interrogation and interruption. "Pete took a beer, and was drinking, and two detectives were observing them in the bushes."

"Those shits!"

"Did you know they passed a law just last week against drinking alcoholic beverages in public places?"

"They did? Last week?"

"At the town council."

And a good law, too, probably, designed to remove this very kind of scum from our local park. "And they were just looking to catch somebody tonight defying the law."

"Yes. Probably."

"And my stupid kid, who doesn't even know there is such a law—"

She looks at me, again with annoyance. "*You* didn't know there was such a law."

"I don't have to know. I don't do my drinking in the park!"

"They put handcuffs on him, marched him and the other boy to a police car, and then searched them."

"They can't do that! They have no right!"

"Pete had in his pocket a small pipe—"

There is a sudden drain of blood from my head, I reach out to the kitchen table top for steadiness. My wife nods. "With marijuana in it."

It is I now, who suddenly feel clubbed. I crumple down into a chair next to my wife, slowly, holding on to the edge of the table. This kid of mine is determined to destroy us all.

My wife continues, her voice a dull monotone. "They're holding him on a misdemeanor charge for drinking in public, and on a felony charge for possession of a controlled substance with intent to sell."

"Oh, no!"

And now, my wife, who up to this moment rather bravely, I think, has managed to hold herself together, suddenly is bent over, her head in her hands between her knees, sobbing. For this alone, I could wring that little bastard's neck. The curve of my wife's back shakes like a bucking horse.

I place the palm of my hand between her shoulder blades. I

should do more, but I don't have the wherewithal at the moment. I am scared. Kids have gone to prison for possession of marijuana. Not as often as formerly, but it still does happen. And with the luck of this family, I know, that is exactly what will happen in this case. My son will go to jail, he will learn all kinds of jailhouse lore, he will be raped, sodomized, turned into a sadist, and will come out spiritually crippled, a resentful thug, and ready to do violence on the world. He will have transformed himself into a fucking little criminal wiseguy. Never again now will he have to play outlaw as a role. He will be one. An outlaw. He will go to prison, and when he gets out and finds he can't get a job, even collecting garbage, he will take himself down to the railroad yards and skulk about with the other hoboes around their bonfires, and when he looks up suspiciously then from the can of cold baked beans he has managed to snitch from the shelf of some Mom & Pop grocery store, it won't be a calculated pose that he strikes any more. It will be an authentic automatic response to a world that he hates, a world that, in turn, loathes him. And his mother and father will go to bed at night, never knowing but what a telephone call will come from the police saying that his body has been found floating in a river somewhere, they *think* it's his body, but they need an identification, because the face has been eaten away by eels.

Well, then, *fuck* him! We deserve better than this! We gave him his chance. And he blew it. Now there is ourselves to think of.

"You have to go down to the police station to sign him out," my wife says.

"Wait a minute," I say. "I don't *have* to do anything."

"The policeman said—"

I interrupt her. "Did he say I would be arrested if I didn't come down to get him?"

There is a look of astonishment now in the smeared wet face of my wife. "They said they would hold him until you came down."

"Good. They can hold him."

"Bill! Your son is in jail!"

"Which is where he belongs!"

"He does not belong there, and you know it!"

I whirl on her. "I do? He's been arrested, Annie—for possession of a controlled substance, with intent to sell. That's criminal behavior. Criminals belong in jail. Or don't you believe that?"

She is up out of the chair, the look of astonishment replaced now by anger. "My son is not a criminal!" she screams.

"*Nobody's* son is a criminal!" I bellow back at her. "The jails are filled with guys like him who are not criminals. They're just no fucking good—either to themselves, or to anybody else. They're bums. Everybody has tried to help them, to give them opportunities, to remove them from temptation, to reason with them, to go hunting in the middle of the night for them, looking under bushes, and being called an asshole because of them. And they go on thumbing their noses at us. People who can't act like civilized human beings don't get treated like civilized human beings."

My wife, though allowing me to finish, is clearly not impressed. "Are you going to leave him in jail?" she asks coldly. Her coldness, I find, is strangely menacing.

"Yes," I say, looking away.

"For how long?"

"I don't know."

The expression on my wife's face is one of disbelief, anger and, yes, even hatred. It is as if I am the beast now suddenly entered into the home, a threat to life itself, an obstacle to be overcome.

Still, it is difficult to say which of us is more threatening to the other at this moment. Perhaps I am more frightened, because behind my anger there is also the sickening realization that in this struggle between us, if I win, I could easily lose her.

I proceed in a more cautious low tone. Excitability, rising easily in me, has been known to raise hysteria in her. "Do you approve of what he's doing?" I ask her.

"Approve?" My low-key approach does not help. She snorts at me contemptuously. It amazes me always how she, for her part, feels no compunction whatsoever against expressing her own feelings in any manner that she wants to. Or is it possible that she is holding back, too, that if not for restraint on her own part, it could be much worse. It's hard to believe. "He made a mistake!" she suddenly hisses at me. "Does he have a right?"

If I say anything at all, I know it will only aggravate her further.

"*You* did crazier things, and you were older!" she spits out at me.

What specifically she is referring to I have no idea. "I was not a dope fiend! I was never arrested!"

"You were hanging out in Paris with that bunch of creeps—"

"They weren't creeps!"

"—Pritch Bates and the rest of them, threatening your parents with giving up your citizenship to become a

Frenchman." She snorts, actually spraying mucous from her nostrils. "You drove your parents crazy!"

"It was youthful idealism!" I roar back at her. "I don't have to apologize for that!"

"Did your father see it that way?!"

"What the hell did my father know?!"

"Nothing!" she screams at me. There is a moment when I actually am concerned that she will assault me. There is a knife on the table. "No more nor less than you do."

"I'm sorry," I say, trying to introduce some dignity in the midst of this maelstrom. "There is no comparison." I catch her eye, and hold it as if in a grip. "My kid is a bum!"

"Oh my God!" If she weren't so angry, it would have come out as a laugh.

Her contempt is infuriating, the fact even that she hardly takes me seriously. I level an accusatory finger at her. "Maybe you think I'm a fool. Peter does. But I've got news for you—and for him. If he wants to go up against me, he'll find he's met his match, babe! I'll squash him like a cockroach, like the little fucking wimp he is!"

"He's not doing it to go against you!" she cries.

"I don't care why he's doing it. He's doing it, and I've had enough of it. I don't go for that crap! It's not *right!* I'm through with him!"

And as I say this, I recognize that I have stepped over a fine line suddenly. It is the end, I have just declared it, there is no turning back, not without a total loss of all dignity, there isn't. Otherwise, all of this thrashing about is nothing but bombast, hollow noise and shouting. It is a commitment I have made, finally, to my own sense of the rightness of things.

And my wife knows this. Strangely, almost as if a burden

has been lifted from her, recognizing that there is no point in continuing to fight, nor in shouting, nor in arguing further, she takes in a deep breath of air. She exhales. She shakes her head sadly, then compresses her lips.

I wait for her to say something, but she doesn't. I study her carefully a moment.

"What?" I say, more quietly. It is difficult to feel comfortable when she turns enigmatic in this way.

"Nothing," she says.

"Oh, yes, something," I say.

She shakes her head again, slowly.

"What?" I repeat.

She says, "You have become the mirror image of your father." I can feel the astonishment leaping into my own face even before she adds, "Only you are worse."

"No! Absolutely not! No!"

"Your father, at his worst, never had the loathsome feelings that you have expressed now to me. As bad as he is, or was, he never, *never* totally lowered the boom on you, did not write you off—"

"It was different!"

She overrides me. "He felt it just as strongly! And he, nevertheless, held himself back! He did not write you off. He never dropped the bomb." Her eyes are burning into me now, as mine did into her a moment or two ago. "And, moroever, you are doing it to everybody." And she crooks a finger into her own breast, and jabs herself hard.

And in that sudden gesture she has just included herself among those who are arrayed against me. It is like a hook in my side. I can't find it within myself even to speak.

"The worst part is," she goes on, her voice growing soft

suddenly and switching now from a tone of anger to one more
of sorrow, "you are destroying yourself."

"No," I say back to her.

She nods. "You are turning yourself into a bitter, defeated
old man, in the guise of some stupid principle, or something.
Some *notion* you have. I wonder if you can imagine how sad it is
to see."

To hear her come out with this, and to feel the full force of
its quiet conviction is like experiencing some kind of death
sentence. Because to deny it simply is not enough. There is too
much truth in it. I do feel nothing but bitterness, hatefulness.
My life is bitter and hateful, and not appreciated. By anyone.
Least of all by myself. There is a moment when I am tempted
to mount some kind of argument in my defense. There are
things that could be said. I could probably say things in my
defense that would wound others. But to what point? To
escalate the argument so as to win her everlasting enmity? "I
don't understand," I say.

And my wife, saying nothing, scrapes her chair over closer
to mine, and facing me, puts a hand on my shoulder, then her
other hand on my other shoulder. She just rests her hands
there, like a mild restraint, waiting. For what? I am not sure,
but I feel the urgency of it.

I don't look into her face immediately. I am looking down
between us. But what I cannot avoid seeing, even there,
staring at the floor, is an inescapable conclusion. "Do I have to
give in on everything?" I say. I look up to face her.

"It's not giving in," she says.

And gazing now into this sad, red, swollen, pleading face,
what I see is the elusive face of dignity that I have been looking

for for I don't know how long. I am holding it in my hands. I bring my face up to hers, feeling the wet cheek against my own.

"All right," I say.

And as I slip my arms around her waist, we cling to each other, I to my salvation, gratefully, having been pulled back, mercifully, I think, from a terrible brink.

We are both jarred in the next instant by the harsh ring of the telephone next to us. Quickly, breaking apart, composing myself, I brush my arm across my face.

"Hello," I say, giving much effort to having my voice come across strong.

"Hello, Bill. How are you?" A friendly voice, but one that I do not immediately recognize.

"Hello?" I say, not letting on immediately that I don't know who it is.

"I saw Tillie tonight." It's my *father,* calling at ten o'clock.

"Oh? Dad! How are you? I didn't recognize your voice at first. You sounded like some young guy." Which is meant to compliment him, of course, but which is also true. His genes are stronger than all of ours put together. And then, "Is Tillie okay?"

"Oh, yes. Fine," he says. "I took her that George Burns book. She's crazy about him, you know."

"Is she reading, and everything?" I am just beginning to breathe easier, relaxed a bit now that I know that the call was not more bad news.

"Oh, yes. She asked for you—and the children. And Annie."

"Oh, good." I'm wondering if this was his first trip to the

hospital to see her. I assume it was. He finally got around to it.

My wife taps me on the shoulder, and says in a husky whisper, "Tell him I sent her a card today."

"Annie sent her a card today," I say.

"Oh, that's good. She'll enjoy that."

"How long will she be in?"

"Just a few more days." A pause. "I'm switching apartments with her."

"What?"

"When she comes home. Well, it'll be easier if she doesn't have to climb the stairs."

I am stunned, knowing how he likes things to remain as they are. "When did you decide on this?"

"Yesterday. I talked with her. Her doctor seemed to think it was a good idea."

"It's very thoughtful, Dad. I know you like your own apartment."

"Oh, the hell with it. It doesn't make any difference to me. This moving is a pain in the ass, though."

"Have you got help?"

"Oh, yes. I've got two kids from across the street. They're doing all the carrying."

There is a moment's pause. "I could come up, if you want."

"No, no," he puts in quickly. "You're a busy guy. You shouldn't take time off." He pauses just long enough to shift gears. "How's Old Pete?"

"Oh, fine," I say. I am tempted to add, Pete's fine, languishing in jail, waiting to get out to lay ambush on us. No, of course, I won't say it.

"Do you think he's on dope?" my father asks, suddenly out of the blue.

"Dope?" I almost choke on the word. "Dope, no. Why?"

"Oh, he just seemed kind of—*sleepy,* when he was up here."

"That's the way teen-agers act these days, Dad. They've got their minds on themselves most of the time."

"Yeah. That's true. I wasn't really worried. Like you say, he's at that age."

I can't help but laugh. "Hey, Dad, what are you becoming, a philosopher in your old age? Middle age, I mean?"

He bangs out a laugh. "Old age, is right. I guess so. Well, you were the same way," he says offhandedly.

"Really?" Did you think I was on dope? That's a new one."

"You were off with the poets there, going to become a Frenchman."

I feel embarrassed. Everybody keeps bringing it up. Do I have to be ashamed of that? It was my revolt, I had to go through it, I shouldn't have to apologize. "Oh, well," I say, dismissing it.

"You had us crazy here for awhile."

I smile. I suppose it is true.

"Pete's just like you," he says.

"Well," I say. And just saying that is enough to let him know I am not really so sure about that.

"Yes," he says. "We're all alike. I was the same way. Sowing wild oats."

"I'm not crazy about the brand of oats they're sowing these days," I say.

"Well, it's true. Everything's crazy. I'm glad I don't have to go through it again. But things straighten out." He coughs out that laugh of his again. "If we don't all kill ourselves first."

Since I don't say anything, he adds, "Don't be too tough on him."

Where is this new mellowness coming from? "How come you didn't take the same attitude toward me?" I put in, the old resentment always gnawing.

"I took it easier on you than you know, kid," he says, with some emphasis.

I don't know why, but it surprises me that he should say such a thing. It is a kind of admission that he once backed down on something. This confession is astonishing to me. More surprising, he seems willing to pursue it further.

"Your mother was pretty good about these things," he says.

I know he's right on that. "Mom was great," I say.

"Yeah," he says in a tired voice. "But don't forget, I listened to what she had to say."

It's true, he did. She was the one person perhaps he did occasionally allow to tell him something. She probably saved him from himself at least once a week during his life. It's easy to forget how important she was to him, how much he must miss her now. Quick to react, slow to understand, nevertheless there was something in him that allowed him to listen, sometimes. Generosity perhaps, as with his giving up his apartment to Tillie. I'm impressed. Perhaps this often undignified gentleman has depths of dignity that he can reach down to and bring up when it's necessary that I have not often appreciated.

"You make a good point, Dad," I say to him, at last.

"I'm a survivor," he says.

"You are," I put in.

"Some of the boys are coming over tomorrow night for pigs' hocks and sauerkraut," he says. "I'm cooking."

"Lucky guys," I say.

"Yeah, well, we'll have some fun."

"Listen," I say, "if you need any help with Tillie, or anything at all—"

"No, no," he interrupts. "Thank you. I appreciate it. But it'll be all right."

"Well, let me know."

"Okay, boy. Just wanted you to know everything's okay."

"Okay, thanks, Dad. Same here."

I hang up, putting the receiver in the cradle lightly, and slowly, and looking over at Annie.

"He's giving Tillie his apartment and taking hers," I say.

"I got that," she says, smiling.

"I'll never understand him," I say. "One minute he can be so totally self-absorbed and insensitive, and the next he can be the most generous and giving guy in the world."

"Like father, like son," she says.

"Get outta here," I say. And after a pause, "Maybe like Pete. What do you think?"

She compresses her lips, vigorously shaking her head no and stomping her foot. She smiles. "That little bastard," she says.

CHAPTER XVII

The police station in our town was moved recently from the basement of Town Hall to more spacious, if somewhat less congruent, quarters in a renovated Victorian mansion on a rise of land overlooking the nearby junior high school. Despite the new exterior of aluminum siding and the paved parking lot filled with black and white police vehicles, from a distance the building retains a look of Victorian elegance, with a three story turret in one corner and gabled windows looking out on an expansive stone veranda. A couple of venerable old maple trees stand on the front lawn that sweeps down the slope below the front of the building.

Once inside the front entrance, however, it is brutally apparent that a trip here is no visit to a Victorian garden party. What once must have been an elegant receiving hall has been karate-chopped into a reception area the size of a doctor's waiting room, with brown linoleum floor covering and naked over-head fluorescent coils, one of which is, in fact, defective and blinking now as I enter.

In the wall opposite the front door there is a double glass window (bullet-proof?) looking in on a small cubicle, which I am not quite sure I should look in on, with a typist's chair and a microphone on a gooseneck armature over some kind of keyboard. The waiting room, which is minimally furnished with three maple chairs and a maple table with some magazines strewn about, is empty. Nor is there anyone behind the window, although I have the feeling they know I'm here because there is a camera at either end of the room attached to the ceiling. Sure enough, even as I am wondering how to announce my presence, an officer in gray uniform (shirtsleeves) appears in the cubicle behind the glass. He is short and fat, and doesn't appear to be in particularly good shape. However, there is a gun strapped to his waist, and judging from a certain swagger about him, he looks as though he would be a tough customer to go up against.

He speaks into the microphone, and there is an electronic amplified voice from somewhere behind me. "Yes?"

I tell him my business, talking at the little perforated metal circle in the glass. I assume that he can hear me, though I am not certain because he doesn't look at me. I explain that I am the father of Peter Brock whom they are holding, I believe. Still without any indication of whether or not he has heard me or knows what I am talking about, he hands me a yellow form to fill out. I have to ask him for a pencil, which he provides through a teller's slot below the window.

The form calls for my name, address, age, and all that, and I attest that I will be responsible for seeing to it that my son appears in Superior Court at such-and-such an address on such-and-such a day four weeks from now at which time a plea of guilty or not guilty may be entered. Sign below. I do, and hand the form back. The officer takes it, and without a word disappears through a door at the back of the cubicle.

I sit down on one of the maple straight chairs in the waiting room, and under the spastic fluorescent coil look over the magazines on the table. There are several well-fingered issues of *Adirondack Life,* a copy of *Today's Motorcyclist* and a six-month-old copy of *Time* magazine. *Adirondack Life* looks pretty good.

It is a long wait. I finish one copy of *Adirondack Life.* A lot of photos of rocks and backpackers. White water rafters. I wouldn't want to take a test on what I have been looking at. You can't help but wonder the whole time you are waiting here what must go on beyond the interior wall of this tiny reception area. Where once the mistress of the house very likely poured after-dinner coffee in the library for the master who then settled into a comfortable chair with a cigar, now there is the starkness of barred cages. Above, where once the master bedroom looked out upon the graceful front lawn, windows are now boarded up, the space partitioned equally into a storage closet for riot guns and a padded interrogation room. One strains to catch sounds of screaming. Whatever they want to do here, you are convinced, they can do it undisturbed behind this wall. It is very humbling.

A door I hadn't even noticed at the far side of the room opens with a click, and another officer in shirtsleeves enters. He is trim, though certainly not undernourished, and wears a Tom Sellek mustache. I rise from my chair, a lot of leather on him creaking and the stiff cord in his trousers making a whipping noise as he approaches. He has my form in his hand, and announces that he is the fink who arrested my son. Though not precisely in those terms. My son and another boy (the latter over sixteen and, therefore, non-juvenile) were observed contrary to Public Ordinance number such-and-such drinking in a public place and further in possession of what appears to be a controlled substance which could constitute a felony, and which is currently being analyzed by the lab (Of course! There is a lab back there. Probably the old breakfast room).

I give the officer my winning look that I gave Mrs. Lacy that says, "I know this was wrong, officer, but you can tell that we're nice people, and perhaps a warning would suffice, and I can assure you it will never happen again." I may actually say some of these things.

This line of bullshit doesn't work on the officer any more than it worked on Mrs. Lacy. He doesn't respond other than to say, "Because your son is only fifteen, you can apply to the court for a juvenile status. Most likely he will be given a term of community service which if completed satisfactorily will then result in the record of arrest being deleted."

"He won't have a police record?"

"If the Court is satisfied that as a juvenile he has been rehabilitated."

Please, dear God, let's rehabilitate him.

The officer takes me back through a labyrinth of corridors and locked metal doors with wire meshed window slits to where they are holding the criminal in a small room resembling a doctor's examining cubicle. He has been fingerprinted, mugshot, and at the moment looks more like a fifteen-year-old wimp than a rebellious hobo. At least, he's scared.

I'm scared, too. Why did the officer bring me back here? There are barred cells across the hall where Peter's companion—the non-juvenile—is now locked up. I hope they throw away the key. Did this cop want to impress upon me the seriousness of the crime? I'm impressed. There are a few other rights and obligations explained to the both of us. I don't get any of it, but I sure will have a lawyer tomorrow make it clear.

After which they let us out, accompanying us back through

the corridor labyrinth, unlocking and carefully re-locking the steel doors, tight security measures in the event that any teenage public beer drinkers might try to make a break for it.

In the front waiting room the officer hands me all the papers he has been talking about, and I thank him. For what? For having busted my kid? I feel foolish and am unable to breathe easy until we are out the front door and free and into the night air again.

The drive home from the police station is not far. Obviously, my kid isn't going to initiate a lot of talk, for which, in a way, I respect him. What's he going to do, try to con me with a lot of chatter? Though I know he must be feeling pretty humiliated. I don't feel like saying a whole lot to him, either. It isn't really necessary to tell him I am angry, sad, disappointed and scared. It will all come out in time. So, uncomfortably, we ride in silence in the dark. I am looking at the road, and he is looking straight ahead, too.

We pull into the driveway, and I shut off the engine, which continues to kick and buck for a minute afterwards, because it is beginning to need some kind of adjustment. Engine run-on, or something, it's called.

Before I get the door handle, my son turns to me, and says in a voice surprisingly clear, "I'm sorry, Dad."

A line like that could open a floodgate of words from me. "Why did you do it?" I say.

"I didn't know there was a law."

"You knew you weren't supposed to leave your room."

"Yeah."

"And the dope?"

"It was just ashes. Old stuff. In the pipe. It was stupid."

I believe him. Old stuff in the pipe. He wasn't *selling* it, for

Christ sake. Stupid bad luck. "Every time you mess around with dope you get banged," I say. "I mean, if nothing else, you gotta understand. That fucking stuff is against the law. They're gonna bust you."

"I know."

"Some guys get away with it, some guys don't." It's even possible there's a note of sympathy in my voice as I add, "Maybe the good guys don't. Is that possible?"

He shrugs. "I dunno. I don't want to get arrested again."

"Or kicked out of school," I put in.

"That's right."

"*Please* don't smoke any more dope for a while, will you? If you want to smoke dope, do it in your room. I'll get mad if I find out, but better me than the cops."

The door to the car on my side is open, and the overhead light is on sufficiently so that I can see him nod, in agreement. I think it's in agreement. There isn't anything more to say, not now, anyway.

My wife is reading the *Times* when we come into the country kitchen/family area. She puts the paper down, folds it over, then looks up at him. She seems to want to say something, but doesn't. Peter stands there awkwardly, his lips compressed.

"I told Dad," he says, "I won't do it again."

She shakes her head slowly at him. I wouldn't want to be him. Well, she shook her head at me earlier. It wasn't so bad. Maybe he'll learn something.

"I broke your window to get in your room," I say to him.

"How come?" he says, probably glad that the conversation is directed away from the more immediate subject at hand.

"Because the door was locked, and there was no answer to my knock."

"Oh," he says.

"You've got mice in there," I say.

"Yeah, I know. They run around at night."

"Why the hell didn't you tell me?"

"They don't bother me."

"Put out traps tomorrow. I'll get some De-con."

He shrugs. "Okay. Can I go to my room now?"

"Probably a good idea," I say.

He bends over his mother and kisses her on the lips, patting her on the shoulder. " 'Night Mom," he says.

"Goodnight," she says. She gives the back of his hand on her shoulder a little pat.

"G'night, Dad," he says.

"Stay in now, will you," I say.

"Don't worry," he says. And goes out.

I look at my wife, and she looks at me. She shakes her head slowly. Who knows?

Two days later my son and I are on our way back up the road along the Housatonic River to his school. His sister has just started fall classes in her own school, the public junior high school that sits within view of the local police station. I had not thought of it before, but that's probably why the cops picked the new location, to better keep an eye on the local beer terrorists.

Following the night of our altercation in the car, my daughter and I both reached the same conclusion, independently, not to pursue it further. She came home early that night, apparently having been too upset to go to the movie. The next day she told her mother that I had acted like a "bully and a beast," but she also admitted under questioning that probably she had

acted in a way as to have contributed her share to the unpleas-
antness, as well.

That was good enough for me. She and I are going on from
here. Without having to say it, she still loves me, I know that.
And she knows how I feel about her. I think my perception of
her has changed slightly, possibly for the better. Perhaps I
respect her a bit more than before. Another blow for women's
lib.

Actually, I'm feeling pretty good about myself today. At the
office yesterday, there was a memo circulated from Frank con-
gratulating "all personnel involved in the arrangements and
preparations" of the Vegas wingding. Apparently the cocktail
party by the pool that I didn't attend was a popular success
with our customers. And the first publicity emanating from
the show turned up as a cover feature story in Larry Hopkins'
The American Review which one of our salesmen got an advance
copy of and sent to Frank. Across the top of the memo sent to
me, I am able to decipher a scribbled note from Frank, one
word: "Good."

Diana Payne-Pignatelli dropped by my cubicle during the
day to comment favorably on my efforts to bring Tony and
Morrie back together. "That was good, Brock," she said.

Good. I'm doing good. Which is what I want to do. I don't
see that Morrie and Tony will ever be friends, but they don't
have to be, really. They are working together. In time, one or
the other will go under, or both will. May the better man win.
Tony tells me, incidentally, that one of the Krauts won the
Vegas raffle, but decided to take the money, instead of the blow
job, then blew it in fifteen minutes at blackjack.

My wife is not with my son and me as we drive back to the
school today. She has a photography assignment this morning.

A family sitting, which will net her $150, and will go into the pot to help pay for my son's schooling. We have to get it up, whether he gets kicked out or not. *He* is paying the $600 for the lawyer who will represent him in Superior Court next month, the money to come from wages I will pay him for jobs that we will find for him to do around the house and yard during vacations. Like scraping the house. I already owe him $150, my wife tells me, for what he has done so far. We are assured that after he has joined the Department of Public Works road crew for forty hours of ditch digging, he will be free and clear of all charges, and as long as he doesn't get busted again, he will not have a police record.

My son has to be back at the school at 9 this morning for a class in algebra. Fifteen minutes away, at 8:30 I catch the news headlines on the radio. The government is still debating whether or not to launch F-111 jets on guerrilla strongholds in the mountains. The news media is not overly critical, but there does seem to be opposition to the idea from some of our staunchest allies. Canada, of all places, has joined with several Organization of American States members to caution against such an attack. No more talk about the Cuban soldiers. Some talk show radio commentator says we have put up with all we can stand, and the time for punitive action is now. I understand the impatience, but on reflection, I don't agree. My wife suggested this morning that we send telegrams to our Congressmen and Senators urging restraint, and I, the professional communicator, did that, reading the message to the telephone operator off the back of an envelope I scribbled it on. I hadn't had my breakfast yet, or even coffee, so it wasn't deathless prose, but it said:

AMERICA THREATENED ONLY BY OWN LACK OF RESTRAINT AND INTOLERANCE TO CHANGING WORLD. WHAT IS REQUIRED IS UNDERSTANDING, NEGOTIATION, COMPROMISE AND COMPASSION. REAL STRENGTH OF THIS NATION IS ITS STRONG TRADITION AND EXAMPLE OF HUMAN DECENCY AND DIGNITY WHICH HAS INSPIRED WORLD FOR OVER 200 YEARS.

It was a little long and wordy, and when it shows up on my phone bill next month will cost a fortune, but it was before breakfast, and my feeling at the time was that after lunch might be too late.

I snap the radio off just as we reach the end of the long driveway up to the administration building at the entrance to the school. It's a good sign, I think, that the government is still thrashing about, unable to decide whatever to do. The car stops, the motor goes off, with the now familiar shudder and shake. I look over at my son. In a little over two years he'll be registering for the draft. I wonder what he thinks about all this turmoil in the world. I have the feeling he is concerned about more immediate matters, what it's going to be like back at school again. To him, two years ahead must seem like eternity. Right now he has an algebra class. So I don't ask him for his opinion on world events. Instead I say, "You gonna be all right now?"

He nods. "I'll be all right," he says.

"Please don't do anything—wrong," I say.

"I won't. I want to get through. Get my diploma. You know, get ready for better things."

"Great," is all I say.

He steps out his side, and reaches in the back for his duffle bag, slinging it over his shoulder, and coming around to my side of the car.

"Get my diploma, man, then go to school for stunt men."

"School for stunt men! They don't have schools for that. You don't go to school for that."

"Well, whatever they have."

"They don't have anything!"

He shrugs, "Well, I'll do it on my own, then." He sticks out a palm for a shake.

"I thought you wanted to do something—*important.*"

"I do," he says. And then, still holding his hand out in front of him, but turning the palm up in a gesture of easy and simple explanation, he adds, "Stunt work is important, Dad."

He flips the hand back to a position to shake again. "So long, Dad. Thanks for—you know—everything. Sorry about it all, but—it'll be all right."

"Will it?" I say, looking him squarely in the face.

He smiles at me. It's that nice smile that never fails to make me feel like I'm going to do something stupid.

"Yeah," he says.

"So long," I say, looking back at him with a kind of wonder. "Good luck."

"Yeah," he says again. "Thanks, Dad. See you." He turns, and with that jaunty hippy way of walking they have, he starts toward one of the other buildings.

A nine o'clock bell rings, and suddenly doors open out of buildings as classes change, and kids come rushing out. My son sees a couple, and waves to them, and they wave back. Stunt school! I start up the car. I'll be late to work, but I'll be there in time for the eleven o'clock staff meeting Frank has called in his office with Morrie and Tony and me.